LAND OF
Lock Down
Presents

LAND OF DA HOOLIGANZ

Against All Odds
PART 3

Written By
IRA B

LAND OF THE HOOLIGANZ 3 | IRA B

Copyright © 2024 IRA B
LAND OF THE HOOLIGANZ 3

All rights reserved. No part of this book may be reproduced in any form or by electronic or mechanical means, including information storage and retrieval systems without permission in writing from the publisher, except by a reviewer who may quote brief passages in review.

First Edition 2024

Printed in the United States of America

This is a work of fiction. Names, characters, places, and incidents either are products of the author's imagination or are used fictitiously. Any similarity to actual events or locales or persons, living or dead, is entirely coincidental.

Lock Down Publications
P.O. Box 944
Stockbridge, GA 30281
www.lockdownpublications.com

Like our page on Facebook: Lock Down Publications
www.facebook.com/lockdownpublications.ldp

Stay Connected with Us!

Text **LOCKDOWN** to 22828 to stay up-to-date with new releases, sneak peaks, contests and more…

Like our page on Facebook:
Lock Down Publications

Join Lock Down Publications/The New Era Reading Group

Visit our website:
www.lockdownpublications.com

Follow us on Instagram:
Lock Down Publications

Email Us: We want to hear from you!

ACKNOWLEDGMENTS

I just wanna say thank you to all those who supported my mission and helped me accomplish my goals as a prolific writer. If you're reading this book then I'm talking about you. Next, Elijah R. Freeman, I tip my hat to you, my nigga. Your pen game is raw, and I appreciate your craft. Tranay Adams, The Realest Killaz series was superb, and it brought back some relating memories. And concluding, I wanna salute everybody else under the LDP umbrella, we are blessed. We are winners, and if it wasn't for the big homie, CA$H, we wouldn't be where we at right now. Keep pushing that pen and stay focused because our stories are changing the book game for the better.

Romell Tukes, SayNoMore, Ghost, Askari, T.J. Edwards, De'Kari and last but not least Aryanna, I'm inspired by your stories, and I hope that one day we can work together on something our readers will love & enjoy. We all we got. Peace.

DEDICATION

I dedicate this book to my sister Brittany and her beloved Sierra. I wish the best in life for the both of y'all. Stay true to yourselves and know that there's more than one street in a relationship. I love you.

Chapter 1

Heaven stared at him blankly for several seconds. Then she went in for the attack. She punched him square in the mouth. She went for his face next, with her nails, and kicked him in the nuts. That sent him buckling at the knees. He grunted and wheezed in pain and agony. Then Heaven drew her Glock .23 and put it against his forehead.

By this time, the other two dudes were drawn down on by the Royals, right there in the corridor of the house. The Royals were ready to dump on them, if they moved wrong.

"You better have one good explanation, nigga," sneered Heaven, her finger caressing the trigger. "Do you know what the hell I just had to go through because I was told Dejah had murdered you, nigga?" she asked.

"So, it was Dejah that killed my brother," he replied.

"I saw her…" Heaven paused instantly, and stared down at the man kneeling before her. It was his statement that made her hesitate and look strange. "I'm not wit' all this bullshit, right now. Who the fuck are you?"

"Can I stand up first?" he asked.

"No. Talk, nigga," Heaven replied.

Wiping his bloody mouth with the back of his hand, the person on bended knee in front of Heaven gazed up at her and said, "Your father, Marlon, was my identical twin brother, who was stolen from our biological mother, forty-four years ago. It wasn't until a few years ago that we finally reunited, and now I'm here to get some answers."

"Did Debra send you here?" asked Leekah.

Hesitantly, he nodded his head. "Yes. She thought it would be best that I approach you, on my own. My name is Kwame Houston. I am the CEO of my own real estate agency. I'm a father and loyal husband, but most of all, I am far from intimidated by whatever you got going on here. I'm here for the same reason you are standing before me with a gun in your hand, the honor of my twin brother, your father. How can we come together to get what we want?"

"And what is that?" asked Heaven.

"Closure," he said.

She frowned. "And what makes you think that's what I want?" said Heaven, refusing to let her guard down.

Without warning, Kwame rose up to all six-foot-two of his stature and stared down at Heaven in quiet interest. She still had her Glock aimed up at his face, one that was uncomfortably identical to her father's, the man whose death had awakened the beast within her. Standing next to their queen, Dyamond and KeKe glared up at the big man, with obvious malice glazed in their eyes. Both Royals were a two man army of their own, and would not hesitate killin' Kwame, if he so much as breathed wrong in their presence, where Heaven's safety was concerned.

"We all desire closure at some point, Heaven," he replied and fought against the discomfort in his genitals. If she had been anybody else, she would have to kill him, because Kwame would have made her pay for that.

"You don't know my desires, nigga."

"But you can share them with me," he replied. "After you put your gun down and welcome me inside."

Heaven held his gaze for a long moment, then she lowered her Glock and said, "What's your name again?"

"Kwame."

"Okay, Kwame. I will let you inside, but don't think just because you're my father's twin brother that shit is sweet here. Don't get it twisted, Kwame."

"I understand," he replied.

With a nod, she stepped aside to allow Kwame to walk past, along with his two companions. Briana, Milkshake and Quana had them under control, as they nudged them forward, with guns at their backs. That's when the total unexpected happened. Suddenly, both Milkshake and Brianna's heads exploded right before Heaven's eyes. Then an arm snaked around Heaven's neck and applied intense pressure, as she then felt the unmistakable presence of a gun pressed against her head.

"Try me and I'll blow her muthafuckin' brains out next," said Rikah, eyeing what was left of the Royals.

They stared back at her in absolute shock and fear for Heaven's life, knowing that Rikah was more than capable of taking it.

"What are you doing, Rikah?" said KeKe.

"Drop them gotdamn guns. Now," Rikah ordered the other four Royals, and Heaven, pressing her body against Heaven's back with her face directly behind her head. "And if you don't think I'm serious," she snarled, before angling the gun against Heaven's head a mere inch aside and squeezing the trigger, as a hot slug grazed Heaven's flesh, causing her to cry out.

That got the other's attention. They dropped their guns at once, seeing the pain written in Heaven's eyes, as her wound slowly bled down her face. Then Rikah made them kick their guns in her direction.

"Now lay down on the floor face down," said Rikah, keeping a strong hold on Heaven's neck.

"I ain't doing all that." Dyamond frowned.

"Your choice." Rikah then shot her in the face, and Dyamond dropped like a bad habit.

When KeKe saw this, she began to panic. Then Rikah said fuck it and killed the remaining Royals. She then eyed Kwame and his two companions, daring them to test her patience. The men got down on the floor facedown. Finally,

Rikah retreated out the front door, with Heaven struggling along with her.

"Me and you are going on a little trip," she said to Heaven, as she forced her up the street to her waiting car.

Heaven said, "And I'm supposed to be scared?"

"You should be."

"I'm not."

"Shut the fuck up," Rikah shoved her pistol into Heaven's back and scanned her surroundings cautiously, as they neared the car parked up the street. That was when it happened. Heaven's whole body locked up, as another one of her seizure episodes began, causing Rikah to panic.

Heaven hit the ground hard, and her convulsions resulting from the seizure had her shaking like she was being electrocuted.

"Shit," was all Rikah could say.

Suddenly gunshots rang out in the night. Rikah looked up and saw Kwame and his two companions running towards her. They were shooting at her, all three of them, making her wish she had killed them, too. Rikah glanced down at Heaven and shot her twice. Then she spun on her heels and took off running.

"Fuck," Rikah screamed into the night. She had failed. Again.

Chapter 2

When the second gunshot exploded, Kiara was through the backdoor instantly. The action was going down, right there in the house, with a dozen cops right outside. Kiara didn't care, though, all she cared about was Jamir's well-being, and that was why she was there right now.

When Kiara made it to the den area of the house, she found two people down. One was Jamir, who was shot in the stomach, and the other was a Royal, whom Toby was standing over with her gun aimed down at her. Then Toby pulled the trigger again, splattering the Royal's brains all across the floor. Although it was dark in the house, Kiara had seen enough to know what was going down. Then Kiara sprang into action, taking the gun away from Toby and telling her to get out.

"For what?" Toby asked.

"Go get Jay help. Go," she said. "Please."

Understanding what was going on at that moment, Toby gazed down at her brother and her heart squeezed with panic. Then she rushed for the front door, unlocked it, and was out of it in a flash. Leaving Jamir there bleeding to death was the hardest thing she had to do, but he needed help, and it was right outside.

"I'm here, baby boy. I got'cha. It's okay. Help is on the way," said Kiara.

She had fallen to her knees beside him and was pressing both hands against his wound.

"Mama," Jamir cried out in pain and agony. "Please," he said, "don't let them… hurt my… mama."

He was lying there, bleeding furiously, and his only concern at that moment was his mother's safety.

"She'll be alright, baby. Try not to talk, okay. Here comes help right now," Kiara assured him.

Then ten seconds later, four uniformed cops came through the door, with a team of paramedics, right behind them.

"I'm not going nowhere, Jay. I promise," said Kiara, when she was told to move aside so the professionals could take over.

By this time, the lights were on in the room and the bloody mess before them all was a very sobering sight to see.

"What happened here?" Asked Officer Wayne Taylor, which was one of the few black cops present.

Kiara's mind was busy trying to concoct a good lie to tell him, so as not to incriminate Toby. Toby did not return. She knew it was best to keep away for now. The stakes were too high, too dangerous.

"Jamir thought he saw somebody over here in the house, when there shouldn't be. I know the person that owns this house. She's my best friend."

"Monica," said officer Taylor.

She nodded. "You know her then," Kiara replied.

He told her to continue, and she did.

"He saw the back door was kicked in and came inside, and that's when she shot him. I shot her next."

"Where did you get the gun?" he asked.

"It's one of my husband's guns," she said. Then she went on to give a plausible excuse why she was carrying a gun, using her son's situation to convince him.

The look of suspicion on his face was clear, but he didn't challenge her on it. Though he did have one of his men dispose of the gun in a plastic evidence bag. For some reason, that action bothered her.

Before long, Jamir was loaded onto a gurney and wheeled out of the house, towards the waiting ambulance. Kiara left the officer standing there, on the front porch, and got into the back of the ambulance with them.

"I'm his mother," Kiara lied to the senior paramedic, who demanded to know who she was.

It was obvious that her presence was not expected, and she didn't give a fuck.

"Just stay put and out of the way, please," the guy said, and Kiara gave a curt nod.

The whole way to the hospital, Kiara held Jamir's hand and spoke to him through his ordeal. At the hospital, he was taken into surgery immediately. She waited outside the operating room door, pacing the floor. Prayer was the only thing she could do for Jamir now. She prayed hard for his life to be spared. The last thing she needed was to lose another one of her babies. Jamir was just as much her son as he was his own biological mother's. He was family, and family was all that mattered. That's when it registered. The dead Royal. She was one of Heaven's girls. *But why shoot Jamir, when they were on the same team?* She wondered. What was really going on within her family circle?

Her thoughts were shattered at the sudden commotion just up the hall, around the corner. Then another team of clinical personnel was rushing up the hall in Kiara's direction. They had someone strapped onto a gurney, hurrying them towards the other operating room.

"Oh my God," Kiara gasped.

Not only was Heaven the person they were pushing past her, but the man rushing alongside of her gurney was Marlon Jones. As they hurried past her, Kiara felt her heart begin to thump rapidly in her chest, with pure astonishment.

Marlon is alive, she thought to herself.

Kiara could not believe what was transpiring right before her eyes.

Up the hallway, into the next operating room, they went. When attempting to follow behind them, Marlon was halted by the ENT, as if deciding to go in after them or not.

"Marlon?" Kiara called out to him.

At the sound of her voice, he turned his gaze on her, and Kiara's breath was stolen away from her. It was him. He had muthafuckin' resurrected, and then he made his way over to her.

"So, you know my brother, too," he said.

"Your brotha?"

He nodded. "Yes. Marlon. He's my twin brother. And you are?" he asked.

Kiara said, "What the hell you talking about, Marlon?"

"I'm not Marlon," he replied.

She opened her mouth to respond, then nothing came out, because all of a sudden, an unexpected discernment of what stood before her left Kiara speechless. She was totally baffled.

Chapter 3

Although she was high as a kite from the blunt she had smoked with Zamon, LaShonda was more focused now than one cared to believe. Her highness only made her more psyched in her zone to wreck some shit.

The Hooliganz already knew what to do, once they reached their location. LaShonda wanted to make Heaven hurt, and she, no doubt, was going to feel this one. Their target was Heaven's truest best friend, Veronica, who still lived in her childhood home with her parents and siblings, despite all the money Heaven had given her. She claimed that she was putting the money towards her plans to jumpstart her own nail salon. Veronica was very independent and blatantly stubborn, and her decision to stay home was about to be her worst one yet.

When the black SUV entered the Lake Skillet neighborhood and turned down Hamilton Street, towards Veronica's house, Zamon and the rest of the Hooliganz readied themselves for action.

"Kill everybody in the house," she replied.

"The kids, too, ma?" Hollow questioned.

"You got a problem wit' that, Hollow?" LaShonda retorted with iciness in her voice.

It was evident that if he did have a problem with it, she would solve it herself. At that point, LaShonda had no understanding whatsoever. Her husband was murdered earlier that night, and she was doing whatever it took to make

Heaven feel her wrath, even if that included fuckin' Hollow up because he had a problem with killing kids.

"Naw," Hollow said slowly. "I'm down for whateva, ma."

LaShonda was far from convinced, because Hollow wouldn't have asked, if he was really down with it. Though all he had to do was give her a reason, and she was going to bust his whole head open.

"Okay then," said LaShonda. "Let's do this shit."

The house in question was at the end of the street, the last house, to be exact. Behind the SUV, in the stolen car, was Erick, another Hooligan, who was riding solo and ready to crush something, too. When they rolled up to a stop outside the house, Zamon, Lil One, and Erick jumped out and headed straight for the front door.

"The fuck you waitin' on, Hollow?" snapped LaShonda, as she exited the truck next.

"Your slow ass," he replied. "You taking your sweet ass time and shit. We on a mission and somebody gotta watch your back out here." Hollow stepped in front of her.

"I got me," she told him.

"Me too, ma," he said. "I gotcha, too."

The Hooliganz had already forced themselves into the house and were setting it off up in there. When LaShonda entered through the front door of the house, everybody in the house was dead, all except Veronica, whom Zamon was dragging by her hair up the hall, into the living room. She was screaming and carrying wildly, causing Lil One to kick her in the mouth to shut her up.

"Don't worry, Veronica, it's about to all be over," said LaShonda.

Then she aimed her gun down at Veronica's fearful face and let that muthafucker rip.

Blocka. Blocka. Blocka.

Three shots to the head was all it took to get the job done. LaShonda looked over at the others and saw them staring at the space where Veronica's face once was. Her body twitched a few times, and then it went suddenly still.

"On to the next one," LaShonda said.

As they all made their way back outside, another car pulled up on the scene. They upped their weapons. That was when two more Hooliganz got out of the car. Both Kweli and Marco were strapped with them bangers, too.

"I see y'all already ten steps ahead, huh?" Marco said.

"This ain't time for social hour," said LaShonda, as she walked right past the two Hooliganz, headed for the truck.

"What's her problem?" said Kweli.

"You don't know?" asked Zamon.

"Know what?"

"They killed her husband t'night," said Lil One.

A minute later, they were back in traffic. Zamon was on the phone with Kweli, who had left the stolen car back at the house, but not before wiping it down quickly and then teaming up with the others. He and Marco were now riding with Erick. Zamon was on the phone getting the scoop on what Marco and Kweli had been up to lately. Then the phone call came through to Hollow from Toby, to inform him on what happened to Jamir.

"Oh shit."

"What?" LaShonda spoke up.

When he told her what Toby shared with him, LaShonda reached for her heart. Then she pointed her gun at him and ordered Hollow to take her straight there. Zamon delivered the information to Marco, and from there, the news was sent through the proper channels to alert the rest of the HCG crew.

At the hospital, LaShonda was escorted up into the spot, like she was Queen Elizabeth. The Hooliganz were moving like they were the Army's infantry team. Then LaShonda go the surprise of her life. The instant she saw Kwame, she immediately came to a halt, her eyes wide with disbelief, her heart thudding with uncontrolled emotions at the sight of him. She blinked twice, swayed on her feet for a second, and then towards him she directed her next course.

He and Kiara, along with Harold and two of his buddies, were all occupying the waiting area of the hospital. When Kwame looked up and saw her coming towards him with six mean looking Hooliganz in pursuit, he rose to his feet and braced himself for action.

Kiara shot up to her feet at once. "Don't," she said to LaShonda. "It's not what you think, LaShonda. He isn't who you think he is."

"What do you mean by that, Kay?"

"He's not Marlon," she said.

"Not Marlon?" LaShonda came to rest before him, and upon further inspection, she could see that what Kiara said was indeed true. The features were shockingly the same as the real Marlon, just not the air of gangsterism and the swag LaShonda always knew him to possess. "If you ain't Marlon, then who the fuck you is?" she asked.

When he opened his mouth to speak, Kwame glanced over her shoulder behind her, and grew very alarmed. Following his gaze, LaShonda looked behind her and automatically knew something was about to go down. A group of Royals had walked through the door and, on sight, them bangers came out. The Hooliganz followed suit and drew their weapons next. Then Kwame took ahold of LaShonda and pulled her behind him protectively. The Royals remained standing in front of the doors. They were looking at Kwame, but watching the Hooliganz, too. His presence was the reason why the Royals had not lit the spot up, like the Fourth of July.

"No, LaShonda," whispered Harold from behind her. He stilled her arm from reaching for her gun.

He knew if she did so, all hell would break loose. It was a Mexican standoff.

"Let me handle it," Kwame replied.

"That won't be wise, Kwame. Just as soon as they see that you're not Marlon for real, it's going down," said Kiara knowingly.

"I still have to try my luck," he said. Kwame turned a humbled glance on LaShonda and said, "Be cool." Then he walked towards the Royals, who stood there firmly and ready.

"Be cool," Harold told her, too.

"I am cool."

"No you ain't," said Harold.

He was scared to release her arm, for fear of her setting it off in there. LaShonda was far from cool. She was hot as fish grease, with blood in her eyes for every single Royal present.

Chapter 4

After the guard had made his ten o'clock round, Delani covered his window and went to retrieve his phone from the hiding place within the bed mattress. He inserted a freshly charged battery and powered it up. He hadn't reached out to the streets all day, so Delani was anticipating his communication with the outside world. Little did he know, there were dozens of missed calls and several text messages waiting for him, when the phone powered on.

"Damn," he said, settling in to review the text messages.

Before he got through the second one, Delani was bolting upright on his bunk and staring at the phone, like it was some alien object. It was a dire message from White Boy Ty, demanding that he call at once. That it was war in the streets and the pressure was coming from in-house. Neglecting the other text messages, Delani went on and called his brother, Ty, to get the lowdown. White Boy Ty answered on the second ring. By this time, Delani's heart was racing.

"Hold up, Dee," Ty said, and was back on a second later, after activating the speaker phone. "I got Toby, Rikah, AV, Peanut and Twan wit' me right now. Yeah. It's up out here, Dee, and we about to turn it up some more."

"I'm listening," said Delani.

Then the most disturbing news next to Vermani's death was dropped on him, like a nuclear bomb. The Hooliganz Crime Gang was going to war with Royal Mafia. His people were out there killing up one another, all because some mysterious Italian bitch shows up with evidence that Dejah and the HCG crew were behind Marlon's death, the second time. But what blew Delani was the situation regarding Jamir's attempted kidnapping, and then Jamir being shot and in critical condition. Tears welled up in Delani's eyes at the thought of losing his little brother. Heaven wasn't playing out there, and Delani knew that she was going to keep turning it up, until she got what she wanted.

"What's the latest on Hev?" Delani asked.

Rikah wasn't sure whether Heaven was dead or not, after she had shot her, just an hour ago. When he heard this, Delani had to catch himself from spazzing out on Rikah. He knew her situation and understood the rules of the game, but Heaven, though? He stressed. Regardless where her heart was at, she was still his beloved little sister.

"Has anyone contacted LJ and Shamar yet?" White Boy Ty asked the question in general.

Delani thought about that for a moment and knew, without a doubt, how Shamar and LJ were going to react to the news. They were going to go ape shit. Delani was almost scared for them to know what was going on, but he had to warn them. So he put a call through to Shamar, first. To Delani's surprise, he was already on the phone with Dejah at that very moment. The lines were all merged together, with LJ included, as everyone was being brought up to beat on everything. Just as they all knew he would, LJ roared like an angry loin, and it took them several minutes to calm him down.

"We gotta remain calm, right now," said Dejah. "We can't afford to lose our cool. We gotta stay sharp."

"Which means we need to pull the crew off the streets, for now, and focus on this plan I got," said Delani.

"You keep talking about this punk ass plan, and not one of us know what the fuck it is, Dee," said LJ with an attitude.

Delani told himself not to feed into it. He knew LJ was just angry, and scared for his family. He just needed to release his frustration in some way.

"I got it taken care of," Delani reassured them all. "All I need for y'all to do is trust me on this. Fall back on that war shit wit' Hev and lay low. I'ma need the crew to make that move in a second," he replied.

"What's a second, Delani?" asked Toby.

He knew what she meant. Toby was his ace, and Delani knew she was missing his presence. They had been a powerful force together, and he longed for that existence again. His plan would definitely make that happen, risky but worth the shot.

"Again, stand down and wait for my call. I know that might sound difficult to do, considering the situation, but I need full respect on that order. Understood?" Delani was now up on his feet in his cell and pacing the floor, as he fought against his own inner beast, threating to be released.

"It's done," said Toby.

"Me too, brah."

"This shit is crazy," LJ bellowed.

Then he disconnected from them, and all Delani could do was shake his head wearily. LJ was going to be a problem, and his rage would be felt sooner than later.

Dejah said, "Cease fire and go underground, right?"

"Yes," Delani sighed. "Please?"

When the rest of the crew assured him that they were going to honor his call, Delani told them all that he loved them and would call back later. After hanging up with them, Delani placed a call through to his loyal source, Nurse Ranaja Brown, someone who had yet to let him down. At that moment, Delani hoped like hell she didn't start now. He needed her like the air he breathed, like his freedom.

"Hello?" came Nurse Brown's groggy voice, answering his call.

"Please tell me you got those names ready for me."

She yawned loudly into the phone. "Yeah," she said, and Delani almost buckled in the knees with relief. "I finished them up earlier this evening, after I got off work."

"Perfect. Now forward all the info to the phone," he told her, with growing excitement.

"That's done already, Delani. Didn't you get my text message?" she asked.

"I prolly did. I ain't got to it yet."

"It's there."

"Thank you, beautiful."

"And Delani?"

"Yeah?"

"After all we've been through already, you still never really asked me why I'm doing what I do for you."

He paused for a second. "No. I didn't. I mean, why are you doing it for me?" he asked with emphasis.

Ranaja also paused for a second before speaking. "Because of how you always held my cousin, Donte, down, when he needed you the most, before he died."

"Donte?"

"Yeah. But y'all know him by Killa Don. He was my big cousin, and he always spoke highly of you. So, that's why I'm doing what I do," said Ranaja. "You kept it real wit' him, so it's only fair I do the same for you, Delani," she expressed.

"That's some real shit, baby," he said.

"I got you," she told him.

Those words were music to Delani's ears. Here it was, his dead homie, Killa Don, was still looking out for the team, even from his grave. It gets no realer than that. Now it was time to really shock the world. He was on his way. Free the Hooliganz Crime Gang.

Chapter 5

After leaving the house to get Jamir help, Toby decided to clear the spot with White Boy Ty. Then Rikah called, and they went to retrieve her from East Quincy. When that mission was accomplished, and Rikah told then what went down back at the house, White Boy Ty spotted AV, Peanut and Twan in traffic, and they reunited at the 24-Hour Kelly Jr. convenience store. There, the team exchanged confidences and politicked on the matters at hand.

Then Delani called, and the order to stand down was given. It was a hard pill to swallow, after all that had transpired throughout the evening, but his authority wasn't to be questioned. For all they knew, Delani's concern was to avoid what could be avoided, so as not to create more damage. If HCG backed off now, that would leave Royal Mafia with no one to strike out against anymore.

It was worth the try, but Heaven was not going to rest until vengeance had been served, that was if she was still alive. But with her dead, shit could get more drastic with her crew. Royal Mafia was a force to be reckoned with. They were vicious, and so were the Hooliganz, whose reputation in the streets paved the way for Royal Mafia to step in.

The crew decided to go check up on Jamir and his situation. They left the store and made their way over to the Quincy Hospital. On their way there, White Boy Ty got the call from Zamon to put him up on game. They too were on their way to the hospital.

"LaShonda?" Rikah gasped in surprised. "Really? Then again, I'm not surprised," she said. "Mama can get a lil gangsta when she wanna."

"From what brah told me, she was on some real deal gutter shit t'night," said Ty.

"Her husband was killed tonight, so that's enough fuel to make her snap the way she did," added AV.

The ride to the hospital was short, but it was what they saw when they got there that made them get their act right. As the car was driving past the front entrance, they recognized a group of Royals posted up inside. From the looks of things, they had their guns out. That was all Toby needed to see to press the brakes and stop the car.

AV was the first one out of the lead car, then Twan and Peanut, along with Rikah and White Boy Ty, all clutching their burners and down to make a move. The Royals were so focused on what was going on in front of them that they failed to see the threat creeping up behind them. That was until one of the Royals, Lele, glanced over her shoulder, just as the Hooliganz were getting in position. Lele said something to the others, and all heads spun in the Hooliganz direction immediately. Now they became frantic and appeared as if they were about to start blazing.

"What's up?" AV said to the Royals, opening out his arms in a challenging gesture.

He and the rest of the Hooliganz just stood there, outside the entrance, waiting to see who was gonna make a move first. Rikah stepped forward, with two guns in her hands, daring them to test her gangsta now.

"Do. Y'all. Hoes. Want. Some. Smoke?" Twan was already amped up after he and Peanut put in that work earlier, on a few Royals downtown.

He was a young, eighteen year old hell-raiser, who didn't give a fuck about nothing. Right then, another person appeared on the other side of the door, and White Boy Ty cussed under his breath. Toby couldn't believe her eyes, but

Rikah was beyond shocked by the face. She upped her tools and was just about to send them hot slugs in his direction.

"Twelve," AV called out. "Heads up."

Instantly, the Hooliganz turned and saw two police cars turning into the hospital's entrance. They lowered their weapons and watched in silent forlorn, as the cruiser made its way in their direction. The second car decided to go another way, to park near the emergency entrance.

"I don't care about them crackaz," said Twan. "Them bitch ass pigs can get the bizness, too."

"Chill out, lil brah," White Boy Ty told him.

He then tucked his burner quickly and told the others to do the same. The lead cop car had two officers inside. The one near the emergency entrance was riding solo. He was already out of his vehicle while the lead car still rolled past the Hooliganz, standing in the parking lot outside the building. Peanut was expecting them to stop right there and get out on their bullshit. They kept right on going, but not without glaring at them, as they stood there on alert.

"Fuck this shit," Toby replied. There was nothing or no one about to stop her from going up into that building. She shrugged her shoulders with nonchalance and pushed forward, headed for the entrance door.

"What seems to be the matter, guys?" said the young white cop, who was approaching the crew.

"Everythang good, officer. No problem," White Boy Ty answered, as he took off after Toby.

If she was going in, then they were going together.

Beyond the entrance door, the Royals had also tucked away their tools, at the sight of the cops, but by now, the pressure was up on whoever else in the building was present to witness the interaction between the two crews. They knew to steer clear out of harm's way. At any given moment, shit could pop off and the result would be just another murder scene to add to the others of the night.

When Toby entered through the door, she intentionally bumped shoulders with Erikah and Nai Nai as she passed. Also, in passing, she grilled Baiyina, whom she knew was calling the shots of their present crew. Every last one of them, Toby had recruited personally. She knew neither of them would get her timing wrong. They knew Toby was an animal and didn't dare challenge her.

Upon her entry, Toby saw more Hooliganz inside, and knew why the Royals had just been in such a frenzy. Hooliganz Crime Gang was up in the building, regulating and ready to get shit poppin' if need be. The rest of the Hooliganz entered cautiously, never taking their eyes from the Royals. The tension was thick. All it took was one mishap, but everybody knew their place, and where one another stood at that moment.

"Hev gotta be in here somewhere," said Toby, as her and Ty walked alongside each other. "That's the only reason I can think of why the shit ain't going down right now. They are here to protect Hev. I know they are."

"And we're here to protect Jay," Ty replied.

Then he shot another lingering look at the Marlon look alike, and knew there had to be a damn good explanation for this. He was the one who assisted in disposing of his body, so that nobody would discover it. Whoever the nigga was, was really freaking White Boy Ty out, on the low.

"Where the hell have y'all been?" LaShonda demanded, once Toby finally made it over to them.

Toby dapped up the other Hooliganz and embraced them with love and respect, before she directed her attention on Jamir's mother.

"The same thing you been doing. I hear," said Toby humbly. "Out hunting and making it do what it do, to put on for my team."

"And what team is that?" LaShonda asked.

Toby frowned at her audacity to question what side she was now on. "The same one that personally saved your son tonight, after them bitches kidnapped him. Don't ever question my loyalty, LaShonda. Real shit, mama."

"Toby," Harold warned her.

LaShonda gave him the hand and told him that it was all good. Then she turned her gaze back on Toby and said, "And I appreciate you for what you did, Toby. Jamir is your baby brotha and I know you'll never do anything intentionally to bring harm against him."

Toby nodded. "Never."

"But what about them though?" said AV, gesturing towards the Royals, who had moved father into the reception area of the hospital.

They kept their distance on the other side of the room, while Baiyina conversed with one of the nurses regarding Heaven's condition. Looks of pure malevolence and loathe were passed between the two groups.

"While we're in this hospital, we are gonna act civilized and behave ourselves, like human beings," said Kiara. "We're not here for all that foolishness."

"Outside the hospital is open season, though," Lil One cut in, and received head nods from his peers.

"Say no more," said Ty. "But there's been an updated memo provided t'night from Delani, himself."

At the mention of her son, Kiara turned to face White Boy Ty with interest. "You spoke with him tonight?"

"Yep."

"What did he say?" she asked.

He told them all that was decided by the big dawg, himself. LaShonda wasn't feeling that at all. She wanted more blood.

Chapter 6

When Jamir was finished with the surgery, and had emerged from the operation room, with another promise at life, he was then transported to his assigned room in the ICU ward. His whole team was right there to support him, and see that he was well protected.

Twenty minutes afterwards, Heaven emerged from the operating room in a coma. Although her surgery had been successful, her condition was still critical, and she was hanging on by a thread. The bullets to her chest and head were a sure death sentence, but Heaven was fighting for her life. She refused to be taken out that easy.

Heaven's condition had moved everybody, even the ones whom she had directed her wrath against, including Da'Jhana, who had heard all about the war between Royal Mafia and Hooliganz Crime Gang. She knew who Heaven was, and had always admired her. Though she didn't know Heaven personally, but through reputation alone. She was one of the younger divas, a shot caller that most of the girls under her always looked up to. But to hear what had happened to her affected Da'Jhana in a way that not even she expected. She felt sorry for Heaven and her family. Da'Jhana could also empathize with Heaven's family because she was going through the same pain and struggle, which seemed to not have an ending.

What she witnessed, her brother being murdered and her big sister being shot, was enough to create hatred in her heart. She knew her brother had died by the hands of a Royal Mafia member. The same Royal had almost killed Tiwanna and took Corey, whom Da'Jhana had written off as being dead now, too, murdered by his own sister, or by whomever his actions had caused to retaliate against him. Da'Jhana blamed Heaven partially for her current anguish. If she hadn't created Royal Mafia then, perhaps, she would still have her big brother and Corey. The same girl she once admired was now an object of her scorn. Da'Jhana wanted so badly to strike back. She was hurting. Badly. While sitting at her sister's bedside, watching as she slept, Da'Jhana wondered how her mother felt now, when she learned about what happened.

Camilla Brooks was a poor excuse for a mother, a shame to her family. All she ever cared about was selling pussy to get money she needed to purchase her fix and a bottle of whiskey. She didn't give a fuck whether it was affecting her children or not. Just as long as she could get her smoke and drink on, nothing else mattered. Now her black ass was sitting in county jail, looking like a dumbass, while her children were out here suffering.

Long ago, Camilla had burned all the bridges with her immediate family, to the point they'd turned their backs on her. That was why no one showed up to offer their love and support when all had failed. Bully Gang were their only support. Their families had been the ones to step up to the plate, them and DaJhana's two most trusted home-girls, Dez and Kyiah. If it wasn't for them, she would have gone crazy by now, and of course, Taquan, too.

The door to the room opened and to Da'Jhana's astonishment, it was Rikah who had entered. She sat upright in her chair and cast a quick cautious glance over at Tiwanna. Her immediate thoughts were to stand up and defend their honor, but something told her to be still. This wasn't time for that.

"How is she doing?" said Rikah. She had entered further into the room and come to rest at the foot of Tiwanna's bed. The look she gave Rikah was icy cold.

"Why should you care? It was one of y'all who had killed my brotha and did this to my sista." DaJhana couldn't help it. She needed to strike out at somebody.

"I understand how you must feel, DaJhana. And I do care," said Rikah.

"Whateva." DaJhana rolled her eyes.

"I do. Tiwanna and I are friends. We went to East Gadsden High together," Rikah admitted

"If she's your friend, then why the hell did you let that bitch do this to her? And kill Broozy?"

"That's because I didn't know until afterwards."

"Whateva."

Rikah sighed and shook her head. She retrieved the cellphone from her jacket pocket and stepped around the bed towards the girl. DaJhana sprung to her feet, with her fists clenched, ready to put hands on Rikah.

"I'm not here to hurt you."

"What're you here for then?" asked DaJhana.

"To bring your heart peace, at least for the moment." Rikah swiped at the phone's screen for a second, then tapped it twice with a finger. "Is this the person you saw kill your brotha and shoot Tiwanna?"

Da'Jhana stared at the screen turned towards her and immediately recognized Baby Gal's face. Then Rikah tapped the screen and, suddenly, the image enlarged, and Da'Jhana nodded her head in answer to the question.

"Watch," said Rikah.

A short video clip began with Baby Gal's murder being the focal point of the matter. At the sight of such cruel actions happening before her eyes, Da'Jhana gasped in horror and turned away from the phone.

"Your brotha's killer is now dead, Da'Jhana."

"Why did you keep…that?" asked Da'Jhana, pointing a finger at the phone, with a disgusted expression on her face.

"Insurance," said Rikah. "Plus, I knew you would want to know what happened, and now you do."

"Why me, though?"

"Why you what, Da'Jhana?"

The girl turned back towards her big sister and stared down at her longingly and saddened.

"Why me?"

Now Rikah was understanding what she was asking and came to stand next to the girl. She laid a comforting arm around her shoulders and pulled her close.

"Because I know what it feels like to lose a big brotha," she said softly. "And I still don't know who took him away from me."

Da'Jhana gazed up at Rikah. She had tears in her eyes.

"I'm good," Rikah sniffled and looked away.

She wasn't good at all, and Da'Jhana could see that clearly. They both were hurting. Shit was deep.

Chapter 7

There were so many cops in the hospital that night that it changed the whole atmosphere. Word got out that HCG and Royal Mafia were at war, and both crews were in the building, at the same damn time. The situation was so critical that the head administrator of the hospital saw to it that both factions were separated. Royal Mafia was on one side of the building, and the Hooliganz on the other side. It had to be this way, or else things could pop off. The tension was thicker than fog. The pressure was on, especially when Monica showed up on the scene, and raised the roof up in that bitch.

LaShonda had already sent word to her that there indeed was smoke in the air, and that she wanted some straightening. Monica sent word right back that she was ready for whatever LaShonda had in mind. When LaShonda called her on it, and was about to make her way around there, it took Kiara and her husband, several Hooliganz, and even Shamar's girl, Danielle, to stop her from going over there.

LaShonda was growing more deranged by the minute. Lisa, who was Jamir's mother-in-law, had shown up with four of her male cousins and big brother. She was there in honor of Jamir, and him being the father of her only grand baby. Plus, a distant relative of hers, by the name of Mildred Andrews, was a local sheriff deputy, and was present to share some much needed information on their current situation. It was hinted that the Feds were rounding up a team to come back down to Quincy to apply some more pressure.

Hearing this only agitated them all, especially the Hooliganz, after having just slipped through their grasp already. White Boy Ty called an emergency meeting with his organization and solidified the order to lay low for now, which meant that they needed to disappear and only move in the shadows, and out of the sight of spectators.

"But what about Jay?" Lil Eddie wanted to know, as AV leaned against him on the far wall of the room.

"I'll have a few men guarding his room in shifts. But for now, I want y'all to lay low," said Ty.

He saw a lot of disapproving expressions, but he knew that none of them would question his authority. He, Hollow, and Toby were now the top chiefs, while the others only served according to their positions and strengths.

"It's not wise for all of us to be here anyway," said Vontay, who was sitting on the foot of Jamir's bed.

Toby agreed.

"We're just sitting ducks to the Feds, in case they want to shut this muthafucker down," said Toby, the instant her cell phone rang.

She pulled it out to see that it was her cousin, Tilly, calling. Toby looked up at Ty and told him who it was. Then she excused herself to take the call in the adjacent bathroom.

"What's up cuz?"

"I got a total of eleven in all, Toby. And Baiyina is the captain right now, with LeLe actin' under her. But it's Skarr who is chief of enforcers now, and she's been given order to go out and recruit," said Tilly, who was older than Toby by two and a half years.

So far, their relation had not been discovered and wasn't a matter of concern, yet Toby was very cautious of that, and was adamant about keeping it under wraps.

Toby said, "Is Skarr around you right now?"

"She's out somewhere with Rhonda and Sophie."

"Find out where they at cuz." Toby knew she had to stop Skarr now, before she added more recruits to their team.

The HCG crew had a total of twenty active members now, and their number should remain the majority.

"How is Jay?"

"A bullet to the gut can't stop that muthafucker, Tilly. He'll be back on his feet in no time. That's a tough one and we're wastin' precious time wit' all this talkin'."

"Right."

"And cuz?"

"Blood is thicker than water. I already know, Toby. You don't even have to worry about that," said Tilly.

She already knew her cousin was gonna say something in regards to that matter and felt the need to say what she said.

"Be careful, my nigga."

"Always."

After hanging up with her cousin, Toby summoned for White Boy Ty and Hollow. They were occupying the small space of the bathroom, within seconds, and Toby shared with them what she learned from Tilly. Without further hesitation, Hollow sent three Hooliganz out to hunt down Skarr and her crew, and put a stop to their mission.

"Tilly will keep you posted. I'm sure?" Ty looked at his woman, and Toby frowned.

"Why ask a question you already know, Ty?"

He threw his hands in surrender and said, "Lemme go clear the room out and set thangs for what we need, in case of emergency."

"Yeah, go do that," Toby retorted.

Ty looked at her oddly. "You okay, baby?"

"I'm good," she lied.

Then Toby eased past him and got out of the bathroom, before he could stop her. With the shake of his head, White Boy Ty sighed and exited the room next. Something was bothering Toby. Something was wrong.

Chapter 8

On the other side of the building, two Royals were posted up outside Heaven's room door. These two were nervous as hell, with the cops crawling about the place, but they still were ready to blaze on a muthafucker if shit got hectic. They were not strapped with their hammers, but they were close by. They were definitely in good reach, in case they were needed to serve their purpose. Can't be too careful, nor too reckless, for that matter. Too much was going on to be slipping.

Inside was Monica, Baiyina, three more Royals, Monique's mother, and Kwame, who was conversing with his two companions, Bobby and Sergio, about what they had just been a witness of, minutes ago, when the Chief of Police had taken out the time to make his presence known. Chief David Monroe was fed up with all the killings and decided to come try to talk some sense into them. They heard him out and Monica kicked him back out the door. It was then that they came to the realization that the street war between Royal Mafia and the Hooliganz Crime Gang was major, so major that the Chief of Police had left the comforts of his own home to come there. So major that he threatened to resign himself from being an officer of the law, if he couldn't bring this war to an end, but he also hinted that he lost a loved one during the madness, and didn't reveal their name. The loss was weighing heavily on him, and the chief was damn near in tears, when he expressed his concerns.

"This shit needs to stop," was his last words, before he finally made his exit from the room.

The whole time, Heaven laid there, still as a corpse as tubes protruded from her body. She looked so frail and broken, but in actuality, Heaven was strong and too stubborn to allow two bullets to do her in. She was a warrior, a beast.

The medical doctors claimed they'd done all that was possible to save her life. It was a waiting game going on now. It was all up to God to do his part. Even if Heaven did pull through, she was gonna wish she had not woken up. Veronica was dead, along with everybody that was in that house with her. They all were gone, except for her big brother, Thump, who was somewhere out of town, taking care of business. He knew now, and Thump was coming full speed ahead with blood in his eyes. That nigga was on some other shit. He had no understanding about the murder of his little sister, father, and his two baby brothers. Thump was about to paint the town red.

But Tabitha was lucky to have survived the hit tonight. She was at work when she got the call about Monique, her brother Randy, and his girlfriend Jill being killed. Monica had sent somebody to retrieve Tabitha from her job at the local senior citizen home. From there she went to her house only to discover a nightmare.

The woman hadn't been right ever since nor would she be for a very long time. Tabitha only had Thump now, and she was waiting for his return. She knew what he was about to do. There was no denying it.

Thump was about to rain Hell down on Earth and nobody was safe.

"I can't just keep sittin' here doing nothin' about this shit," said Monica. She then shot up to her feet and made her way for the door.

"Whoa. Wait a minute, Monica." Kwame reached out to take her by the arm. "We talked about this," he said.

"Don't touch me," she growled up at him, with fire in her eyes, daring him to touch her again.

"Where are you going?" asked Kwame.

She had been sitting over in a corner chair by the window, rocking back and forth, crying quietly and in distress over her dead brother and daughter.

"I'm gonna go get some straightening," said Monica. "My baby is laying there in a fuckin' coma behind this mess, and I refuse to not do somethin' about it," she stated.

"What're you gonna do?"

"Yeah," said Bobby, a forty something nigga with thick eyebrows and a sharp chin. "What you gonna do, Monica?"

Monica glared from him back to Kwame and said, "This is real family business. I don't need nobody following me or intervening in what the hell I'm doing."

"You're not going over there by yourself," said Baiyina.

"You don't tell me what the hell to do, little girl," she frowned.

"I said what I said," Baiyina shrugged.

"And I said what the hell I said, now excuse me!" Monica stiff-armed Baiyina and moved her to the side to get to the door.

She reached it and snatched the door opened, and then she stopped in her tracks at who she saw standing before her. India and Myrical, the two Royals who were guarding the door outside, were blocking the path of none other than Levi Dawson himself. This was the so-called best friend of her former fiancé, Ced, the Fed, who had played Monica for a fool, and now here he was showing back up in her life like shit was cool.

"Let him through," said Monica.

She retreated backwards a few steps to allow him room to enter. Baiyina came to stand next to her, as she watched Levi, without questioning who he was. When Levi was allowed to enter, Monica snatched Baiyina's gun, which had been tucked underneath her shirt. Then she rushed Levi and gripped him by the throat, slamming him back against the wall, and placing the gun to his left temple.

"You got me fucked up, showing your face right now after you and that bitch ass nigga betrayed me," said Monica, sneering up into his wide-eyed expression.

"I think you need to hear this," he replied.

"You got nothing to say to me."

Levi nodded. "You need to hear what I have to say, Monica. I'm not bullshittin' you."

Monica snarled, like an angry hyena.

"Let him speak," said Kwame.

"Shut the fuck up," Baiyina told him, feeling some type of way about how Monica had just jacked her for her hammer.

Then she grabbed Levi by his shirt collar and pulled him further into the room. "Let's see what you have to say, because if it's bullshit, then you'll be the next muthafucker that's gonna need to see a doctor," she said.

"Or a mortician," added Monica.

"It's about Heaven," Levi replied.

"What about her?"

Before he could respond, there was a loud commotion outside the door. Then there was a struggle, and then the unmistakable blast of a gunshot that startled everybody. Then it was total pandemonium in the building.

Chapter 9

His name was Barthrow Kyles. He was an avid hunter and a damn good mechanic, when you needed one, but to the Hooliganz, he was always Uncle Bart, who was White Boy Ty's favorite uncle and mentor. That night, Bart was just finishing up his task of working on a customer's boat engine in his work shed. He shut off the lights when he sensed something. He had just stepped foot out of the shed, when he heard Sheba growling. Sheba was his faithful German shepherd, and she, too, sensed the threat lurking in the night. Uncle Bart laid a hand on top of her head and stroked it gently to calm her down. Somebody was out there, who didn't belong there, and that put them in violation.

Easing back inside the darkness of the workshop, Uncle Bart used his sharp instincts to feel his way around blindly. He knew the space so well that he didn't need light to see. When he made it to the tool counter, he selected a heavy duty wrench and quietly exited the shed again, just in time to see movement progressing near the back of the house. Whoever it was lurking in the shadows around his house was no friend of his. Those who actually knew him knew better than to be creeping around where he laid his head at night.

It was so dark behind the house that whoever it was violating didn't see him easing up on them from behind. Uncle Bart watched as they checked the doorknob on the backdoor and found it unlocked. They eased through the door quietly, a moment later, and Uncle Bart knew it wouldn't be long now. Rocko wasn't going for it. Almost fifteen seconds had passed before Uncle Bart heard a petrified cry come from the house. Then he snapped his fingers and Sheba shot forward instantly. She ran for the backdoor, with Uncle Bart right behind her. For a big stocky fifty year old white man with a bad knee, he sure was moving faster than one would have expected.

When Sheba cleared the backdoor, moments later, another cry exploded from inside. Apparently, her and her brother, Rocko, were getting down to business. With their sizes and both of them on you at the same time, you were in some serious trouble. Uncle Bart entered the house to not only find one of the Royals having been ripped in two, but one whom he would have never in a million years expected to see at that moment.

"Oh, Gucci," he said disappointedly.

Lying on the floor of the hallway, outside the home study of the house, Gucci stared up at him with cold fear in her brown eyes. Rocko had her pinned down to the floor, with his large mouth wrapped around her throat. He was about to rip her throat out, just before Uncle Bart showed up. Sheba was already clamped down onto Gucci's arm, rendering it useless, as she dared not move a muscle.

Gucci was in dark fear that could not be denied, and Uncle Bart almost felt sorry for her.

"Release," said Uncle Bart.

Reluctantly, both dogs backed away from Gucci, who then let out a startling breath and an agonizing groan. She was shaking like she was cold. Apparently, Gucci had not experienced such closeness to death before, especially not with animals, for that matter. One look at Rocko and Sheba glaring down at her was another raw fear that shook her to the core.

"What were you thinking?" Uncle Bart said to her.

"They coming for you," said Gucci painfully. "I came to warn you, Bart," she winced.

He gave her a hard look. "You came to warn me? By sneakin' around my property, like some cat burglar?" he demanded.

"Because." Gucci paused for a moment.

"Because what, Gucci?"

"They already out front waitin'," she said.

Upon hearing this, the old white man looked up towards the front of the house. Then he told the dogs to watch her, while he went to check out things. The house was dark as night, except the lights in the kitchen and the bathroom. When passing through those two areas, he did it quickly, and entered the living room with the quietness of a ghost.

Gucci knew he had two vicious dogs that knew her well, but tonight the situation was different. She made herself the target for destruction by her unexpected actions. Therefore, Uncle Bart would treat her as a foe, until he was convinced that she was actually looking out for his best interest.

In the living room, Uncle Bart eased over to the front window to look outside. At first, he didn't spot anything out of the ordinary. Then he saw the unfamiliar car across the street, just three houses up the street. Two people stood outside the car, waiting for some action, and ready to get active.

"Bart?" Gucci called out to him.

Frowning, Uncle Bart stared out for another moment, then retraced his steps to where he left Gucci. Now Sheba was standing over her head, glaring down into her face. The look the older man saw on Gucci's face was one of pure fright, and a sense of helplessness.

"What are y'all planning to do to me? I thought you and my nephew were family, Gucci."

"We are family," she said.

"Then what is all this about?"

As briefly and painfully as she could put it, Gucci gave him the real lowdown. He listened to her without interruption. Then Rocko gave his master a look, as if to ask him did he believe the bullshit or not.

"I can help you stop them," said Gucci uncomfortably, not daring to move for fear of Sheba tearing into her flesh again.

Gucci was hurting and bleeding everywhere already.

"How?" asked Uncle Bart.

Minutes later, after running down her plan of attack, Gucci found herself at the front door of the house. She was now standing out on the front doorstep and giving the two Royals the signal they were waiting for. Prior to their reaching the house, Gucci had warned the two Royals about Uncle Bart's dogs. She explained that if they wanted to make a successful mission, without the dogs warning the old man first, she would have to go in first, since she already had a good rapport with the animals. That turned out to be a lie Gucci provided at the risk of her enduring what she had just gone through to warn Uncle Bart before the others came, to prove where her love and loyalty truly stood, at that point. So, when the two Royals made their way over and into the house behind Gucci, she led them right into their traps. Tori, one of the Royals, had noticed Gucci's injured arm and had stopped her to inquire about it.

"I wasn't so lucky, at the beginning, wit' them two gotdamn beasts," groaned Gucci in discomfort.

"So, where they at now?" asked Diva, the other Royal, who was recently recruited a couple weeks ago.

Diva was a super thick redbone bitch with a mean murder game and her finesse was superb.

"Where they at?" said Gucci slowly.

"Hell yeah," the two Royals said in unison.

"I locked them in the shed out back."

"And where the old man at?"

Putting her finger to her lips, Gucci said, "I had to knock his big ass out, but I left him back here." Then she beckoned them to follow her towards the back of the house. In her mind, Gucci knew she had teamed up with two of the dumbest bitches in the crew.

Moments later, Gucci led them both down the short hallway, into the second door on their right. The instant Gucci entered the master bedroom, she stopped in her tracks. Tori was right behind her, with Diva taking up the rear. Diva did not see Uncle Bart coming up behind her with the heavy wrench in his hand. She had turned her head, at the sound of movement, a split second before the wrench bashed her across the face.

"What the…?" Tori was then knocked forward by Diva's body colliding into hers, but Gucci was already delivering a vicious jab to her face and slamming her down onto the bedroom floor. That's when Sheba and Rocko came out of nowhere to help Gucci subdue her, now former, Royal sister. Those two dogs sure knew how to latch onto a muthafucker and not let them go for nothing. You could hear Diva scream from there to Miami. Gucci knew he pain. She too was a victim of their wrath. Luckily for her, she was no longer their food.

During this time, Uncle Bart was working Tori over with the big wrench. He was literally reconstructing her face and cracking her skull in. She had already been dead by the second blow and here it was Uncle Bart was already in the double digits. Total overkill. Rage will do that to you.

Chapter 10

The HGC crew had just exited the building when Thump and one of his closest homies had stormed through the entrance door. The only ones left to watch over Jamir were Zamon, Kweli, and little Peanut. They would keep watch during the first shift, while the others went out and did what they were instructed to do, lay low and stay put. Anyone who opposed or disregarded the warning and violated this call would be subject to demotion or, possibly, death. The future of the Hooliganz Crime Gang and the freedom of the ones incarcerated at the moment were riding on their cooperation and willingness to remain humble, all due to the plan, Delani's plan.

But when gunshots rang out in the building, the Hooliganz instantly prepared themselves for war. Zamon took ahold of LaShonda's hand and guided her farther away from the door and to the back of the room. Both Harold and Preach shielded themselves before Kiara and Lisa, while Peanut hurried over to the door to peer outside.

"Watch ya head," Zamon warned.

Peanut didn't just stick his head out the door, but his whole body as well. He stepped outside into the hallway and shut the door behind him.

"Kweli," Zamon called out firmly.

"I got 'im, brah." Kweli moved towards the door next, and just as he reached to open it, Peanut was rushing back inside with a look of alarm on his face. When LaShonda saw this, she demanded to know what was going on out there, with all the running and screaming.

"They're all going towards Hev's room," he said. "But they also running from that direction, too."

"Could be a diversion," said Zamon cautiously. "Create a scene somewhere else that'll make everybody focus their attention on that. Then come and try some slick shit here, but I got that act right for they asses, if they try running up on this muthafucker." He drew both of his Glocks.

"I don't think that's it, Zee," Kweli said.

"What else could it be then?"

No one else had an answer for him. They waited. The Hooliganz, along with Preach and LaShonda, were clutching on their guns and anxiously waiting to see what happened next. There were no more gunshots, only three had sounded off, and then no more after that. Just those three alone were enough to worry about and brace one's self for whatever transpired after that. No one breathed a word for the next minute or two. They were listening, thinking, and anticipating the unknown that was a result of the commotion around them. Then, suddenly, a code knock sounded off at the door that the three Hooliganz knew all too well. Then the door opened and Rikah entered the room. A few breaths of relief were released at the sight of her.

"What's going on out there?" asked Harold, beating all of them to the punch.

"That's Thump around there," said Rikah. She told them what little she knew of the situation, which she'd learned from a few of those who witnessed it. Thump showed up to Heaven's room door, with Meechie, and was blocked from entering by two Royals. Next thing they knew, Thump swung on one of the Royals, knocking them out cold. Then the other reached for her gun, prompting Meechie to bust her ass with three slugs to the chest.

"That damned fool," muttered LaShonda.

"The crazy thang about it, though, is that Meechie is licensed to carry a gun," said Rikah knowledgeably. "By them reachin' first, him killin' her ass will be labeled self-defense. I'll put my money on that," she added.

"That still won't stop him from being a target for Royal Mafia now, too," said Preach.

"The more of them bitches die, the less we gotta deal wit'em," Peanut chimed in. He was so stressed out that he lit a cigarette right there in the hospital room.

"I wanna go over there," LaShonda replied.

"Go where?"

"Where else, Kay? I can't keep this front no more. That's our family round there, y'all. Somebody gotta do something about all this shit, one way or another."

"You sure you really want to do that?" Zamon gave LaShonda a quiet look that spoke a truth of its own.

LaShonda exchanged a guilty look with him, and just shook her head. He was referring to the destruction they'd already made in her wake of retaliation against those who hurt her family.

"Something gotta give though, Zee."

He nodded.

"And where did everybody go?" asked Rikah.

"Oh, you didn't get the new memo? Where the hell you been, when Ty gave the order, per Delani's call?" asked Kweli.

"What's the order?" she said.

It was Kiara who spoke up and told Rikah what her son wanted. Rikah heard her loud and clear, and knew, without a shadow of doubt, Delani had indeed meant what he said when contact with him was made earlier.

"I'm down for all of that," Rikah replied. "I just hope whateva this so-called plan Dee keeps going on about work out for him and the team."

"It will," said Kiara, with true confidence.

"You know this plan my brotha got cookin', Mama Kay?"

"Not any particulars, no," she said. Kiara then took her husband by the hand. "But what I do know is that I no longer feel safe in this hospital."

With that being said, Harold gathered up his wife and her things, and together, they saw their way out, along with Preach, his usual impassive demeanor leading the way. After they left, it was the Hooliganz and LaShonda remaining in the room, watching over Jamir. If anything, the five of them would stand firm against the storm. They would definitely rise up against all odds, and for the remainder of the night, that's exactly what they did, as the rest of the world around them undertook their own persona hardships. So much shit was going on in the world. So much hatred and pain. So much pride, which was the main thing that was getting a muthafucker murdered on every corner. Their pride, one of the worst things a person could ever possess.

Chapter 11

Going underground was perhaps one of the best things Hooliganz Crime Gang had done. With the town being under siege, damn near every cop in the county was locking everything down as a result of the killings. Movement was limited without the law being applied and brutalized. Since HCG was nowhere to be found, the authorities focused their attention on the Royals.

While Heaven was down, in her coma, her empire was changing, and not for the better. With Baiyina calling all the shots, nothing was going as it should, and now there was conflict in the house. When a few Royals found themselves in jail on some reckless behavior, Skarr went out and recruited six more to fill the void. Her pickings were not based according to the qualifications, which Royal Mafia was designed. Within a week's time, Skarr saw just how bad her pickings were, when four out of the nine she recruited ended up dead. Heaven would have been very disappointed. Maybe Skarr woulda died for choosing so poorly, because all she did was basically pick "females."

After several days of being heavily sedated, Jamir was back conscious, but enduring a whole lot of pain and discomfort. During precious moments shared with his mother, she told him all about her journey after Tony's death. To hear that his mother was out there thuggin' with the Hooliganz was something way beyond his wildest imagination.

Through trial and error, Jamir's determination to get better strengthened his will power, because when it was time to bury his father, Jamir was determined to be one of the pallbearers to carry him on his final journey. And that he did, along with his Hooliganz. Jamir stood firmly under the weight of his distress, and pushed forward. That day, Jamir was applauded for his devotion. Because most of the Hooliganz never had a father figure in their lives, Tony had been filling that void, where his love and respect for them would forever carry on. After the funeral, the Hooliganz went back underground, and did not come back out for nothing, except for a few, who were always there to assist Jamir and make sure he was well protected, during his final healing process.

Meanwhile, Monica was losing herself over Heaven's situation, and she was falling hard. The only people who kept her sane were Kwame and Ella Mae, and of course, Anya, along with little Aliyah Renee and Malik, all of whom Monica had no choice but to be grateful for.

As for the story with Kwame Houston, it was quite intriguing and heartfelt, to say the least. He was from Harlem, New York, born from a sixteen year old, who planned to give him and his twin brother up for adoption. But she ended up dying right on the delivery table, anyway. The girl was a runaway, with no next of kin to speak on her behalf, or take guardianship of the twins. Her name had been Chasity Wright, a young girl with potential, ambitious, but yet her young life ended suddenly.

During that same time, Mary Ann Jones was in Harlem, New York, far away from her own small town of Quincy, Florida. She had followed a cousin up there, whose dreams of becoming a model turned out to be lead roles on adult films. Fortunately for Mary Ann, she had found honest work as a professional chef in one of the finest five star diners in the city. That's where she met Chasity, five months prior to her death. The girl had been sleeping on the streets, while pregnant, and Mary Ann took her in.

For the next several months, they established a love-hate relationship, all the way until her final breath in the delivery room. After several days of wrestling with the thoughts of the twins going into the system, Mary Ann came up with a plan to take them both herself. She felt obligated to care for them, which was what she had been trying to convince Chasity to do, but Chasity was not ready for that type of responsibility. She was practically still a child herself, and a very stubborn one.

The day Mary Ann decided to take the twins, in the process of doing so, just when she had one of them secured in her possession, one of the hospital's nursery nurses caught her in the act. Mary Ann knocked her old ass down and escaped with just one of the babies. Two months later, she returned back home to Quincy, where she raised Marlon. Then she had Chad, a couple years later, and raised both of them as best as she could. By this time, Kwame had been adopted and was brought up by two adopted parents, in East Orange, New Jersey, the very same place where he created his own family and made a good life for himself. Then he met Marlon through Debra, after he had sold a house to one of her dear friends. The reunion of him and his twin brother was filled with pain and regrets. Then Marlon got himself killed. Now Kwame was there to get answers, only to find himself receiving more than he bargained for.

This was the same story he had told Kiara and LaShonda, and several others, who cared to listen and had grown close to in the short time he had been there. After surviving two weeks of the mess Royal Mafia and HCG had created around their whole existence, Kwame returned back home to New Jersey, where his own family was. With the time he'd spent amongst the broken blended family of both empires, a lot of them were saddened to see him go. But before leaving, he made an attempt to bring Monica and LaShonda back together, to try and mend their friendship. Both women were too stubborn to make the initial meeting, which turned out to be an exhausting feat for him. So he took his leave, with the hopes of returning back soon to learn that they'd rekindled their bond.

In the wake of leaving, Debra had made her presence known to Monica, with the offer to help, if she desired for it. Her loyalty and devotion was to Marlon, which followed down to Heaven, and now Jamir, whom she, too, wanted them to kiss and make up. Jamir had been totally blown by the truth of the matter that Marlon had been his biological father, and now that put him and LaShonda at odds. Jamir blamed his mother for all the pain and failures he had endured throughout his childhood. He felt, if he had known the truth about Marlon, then his life would have been a lot more meaningful.

"And what about Tony, Jay?" LaShonda had said to him, when Jamir had turned his back on her to walk away, before he disrespected her for betraying his trust.

Jamir stopped in his tracks, just as he was about to shut the front door behind him. "Tony was my father, and he will always be my father. He did somethin' not even your own father was man enough to do," he said. Then Jamir slammed the door behind him, and never returned back to her house.

LaShonda cried like a heartbroken baby after that, scared that she had just lost her child, too.

After two weeks since the war, the streets of Quincy were gradually coming back to life, and Heaven was still in her coma. Royal Mafia was becoming a problem, and Baiyina was beginning to feel she'd bit off more than she could chew. Not everybody was fit to rule, especially now, after Toby and Rikah had taken all of Royal Mafia's product, clientele, suppliers, and the ledger and money. Baiyina could not fully support the team without its proper essentials. Toby had hit Royal Mafia in the pockets, forcing its newly appointed ruler to start from scratch to rebuild their financial support system.

The only money they had couldn't be touched, which was the millions that Heaven had stashed, and only she knew where it was. That led Baiyina to jacking niggas and running money schemes to get their bank back up and proper. Other Royals were falling back, doing their own thing, while Baiyina worked it all out on her own. In the process, the Hooliganz were suspected to have lost their stronghold, but were still running their operation in silence, without it being seen. Jamir was back in position, with White Boy Ty and Toby backing him. On top of that, the HCG was steady growing, and Delani's plan was being put in motion. This was about to be something major, very strategic shit, and nothing was going to stop it from happening. Delani was about to really do it big this time. Free the Hooliganz. Free at last.

Chapter 12

On the morning of the sixteenth day after the Hooliganz had gone underground, Kiara had gotten an unexpected visit by the police. The second she opened the front door, there stood two police officers and a homicide detective. She was handcuffed, read her rights, and escorted to a waiting patrol car. During this time, Harold was out back working on his project of rebuilding the back porch. When he heard his wife cry out to him, he dropped everything and came running. By the time he made it around front, they were already putting her in the backseat of the patrol car.

"What's going on? Why are you arresting my wife?" Harold confronted the detective, who was standing nearby, watching the process of Kiara's arrest take place.

"Murder," said Detective Emmanuel Edmonds, a short, slender, black guy, with a Marine cut.

"Murder?" Harold paused briefly. "My wife ain't killed nobody," he said. "She didn't kill nobody."

"Sure, she didn't," said the detective, in a mocking tone, and left Harold standing there, looking stuck on stupid, as he went for his unmarked vehicle.

One look at his wife sitting in the backseat of the police cruiser, and seeing the scared look on her face, Harold felt his heart shatter to pieces. Then a tear rolled down her face, before Kiara was driven away. At that moment, Harold felt like he couldn't breathe. Then he called Angie Galloway, and she got on top of things, immediately.

"They're charging her wit' two murders in connection wit' the gun that was taken from her the night Jamir was shot. That murder she was not charged wit', but after ballistics on the gun came back from the lab, it was confirmed that two others were killed by the same gun," said Detective Galloway, sometime later that afternoon.

"She didn't kill those people," Harold said.

"She told authorities the gun belongs to you, that night she claimed she killed Heather Peacock."

"I know," he stressed. "She told me."

"Was it yours, Harold?"

He shook his head no. "It wasn't mines," he said. Then he went on to tell her how Kiara actually came about possessing the gun, that night Tony was killed. Kiara told him everything that transpired that night, and now her actions were about to cost her greatly.

"So, the gun was Toby's all along?"

Harold shrugged.

"Then we need to find her as quickly as we can, so she can own up to her bullshit."

"And you really think that's gonna happen?" Harold retorted, with a hint of doubt in his tone.

"Do you want my cousin to go down for this?"

"Hell nawl," he said.

"Then you make her do what's need to be done, Harold. This is serious business. Kiara won't survive in prison. She ain't built for that kinda pressure," she said.

Angie was absolutely right. Kiara wouldn't make it in jail, with her charge. With a murder under her belt, she would, no doubt, be tested and challenged at every turn. The pressure that would come her way would break her. When Harold was done seeing Angie at the station, he went out and looked for Toby.

"I don't know where she's at," said Vontay, when Harold found him and his girlfriend, Armani, at the BP gas station, an hour later.

"But you got her number, right?"

"I got it, yeah."

"I need that," said Harold.

Reluctantly, Harold was given the number. He called her right then and there. The call went straight to voicemail, so he tried it again. When it did it a second time, Harold cussed under his breath and tried it a third time.

"What's going on wit' you, big dawg?" Asked Vontay.

"My wife's in jail," he said.

"And what that gotta do wit' Toby?"

Harold didn't answer the question right away. Then he told Vontay to just let Toby know that he was checking for her, and that she needed to get at him pronto. Afterwards, Harold found himself back in traffic, contemplating reaching out to Jamir next, because if anybody, he would know how to reach her. But Jamir was gone so far underground that not even his own mother could reach him. It was by sheer luck that he bumped into Vontay just now, because none of the other Hooliganz were reachable. Their absence in the trenches was felt. That was not normal.

Hooliganz Crime Gang had literally owned the streets of Quincy, and its surrounding areas, once upon a time. Then Royal Mafia came and changed that course. Then the HCG organization was reborn and reclaimed its rightful status, and now they were existent only in the shadows. So, Harold did the next best thing that was warranted of him, at that point. He went to hire the best legal attorney his money could buy. One thing about Delani, he was very determined to see that his family was financial stable. Harold and Kiara hadn't needed for anything for quite a while because Delani saw to it that they had plenty of money.

He went back home and collected twenty thousand dollars from the safe, and dropped it on the desk of Vivian Evanovich, the president of her own law firm, and daughter of a judge.

"Have a seat, Mr. Bradwell," she offered.

He did as he was told. Then she brought a bottle of cognac from her minibar and poured them both glasses of the brown substance.

"Now tell me everything I need to know," said Vivian.

Harold did that, too. The man was on the verge of losing his head. Kiara was his world, his everything, and now she was gone.

Chapter 13

A few days went by before the news of Kiara's arrest had gotten around to Toby. She didn't need to know who the two murder victims were, before she killed Heather that night. Now Kiara was being charged with Pumpkin and Meesha's murders because she had taken her gun away that night, trying to save her, but still got fucked up in the process.

White Boy Ty worried about Toby's reaction to what had happened with Kiara. He was afraid Toby was considering actually turning herself in to save Delani's mother. Toby didn't want to talk about it. She was mulling on it, and Kiara was suffering right now because of her. That woman has had the worst of luck lately, and then she received the unexpected call from a very unexpected individual, just when things were getting heavy on the home front. She got the call from Sheena Lovette, someone whom she had forgotten all about, until that moment.

"I'm at the Greyhound station in Tallahassee," said Sheena, who too was just released from prison. This was one of the women Redd had told her all about, and Dejah, and now Toby, was about to finally see how she was really living.

Toby went to retrieve Sheena from the bus station. She welcomed her with a nice care package and the key to Redd's old apartment in Tallahassee. There, at the apartment, the two women rolled up a blunt and popped the cork on a bottle of champagne. In the process, Sheena was wondering where Red was. According to her, Redd advised her that, if she couldn't reach her or Heaven, to call Toby, and she would be taken care of her. Toby was doing exactly that, honoring her through Redd's death.

"Redd is dead, Sheena," she went on and said it.

"What?"

When Sheena asked for her to elaborate, Toby did so, and told her everything. On top of that, she told her what was going on at the moment with the family. Toby wanted Sheena to be aware of everything that was going on, so she could decide whether this was what she still wanted or not.

"I'm here now," said Sheena. "So, I may as well make the best of it."

"I'm used to the smoke," she told her, as she fought back the tears that threatened to spill from her eyes. Sheena said, "Plus, I don't have nowhere else to go, Toby, and I'm not going back home to Alabama again."

"This can be your home now, baby."

Sheena nodded her head.

"But you know there's a trial run you're gonna have to go through to convince me and my team you're ready."

"I'm ready."

"Okay. Then I got a mission for you."

"What is it?" Sheena asked.

"A breakout."

"A breakout?" Sheena looked at her oddly.

That's when Toby filled her in on Delani's plan, already knowing that Sheena would do her part well. Still, Toby wanted to see her get down in action, before she brought her to the rest of the team, because Rikah and the rest of the Hooliganz were damn sure going to test her gangsta.

That following week, Tootsie was set free from behind the wall, after ten years of hard time. This was the other prospect Redd spoke on, and Tootsie got the same treatment as Sheena had. Fifty thousand, her own place and car, weapons, and a strong team standing behind her. Sheena had earned her place in the crew, and the Hooliganz loved her.

She and Hollow clicked tight, almost from the start, and so they became their own personalized team. Lil One snatched Tootsie up, off rip, and she was impressed by his young swag and his gangsta, but Zamon put a stop to their budding acquaintanceship, and refocused them on the plan at hand. It was almost crunch time, and everybody needed to be on one accord, when the time came.

"Are we really about to do this, or am I being tested right now?" asked Tootsie.

"Let me tell you this much, Toot," said Sheena, as they both sat together in her Acura NSX, sharing a blunt and their reclaimed freedom. "You've already passed the test last night, when you went up against Rikah, without knowin' who she was. All Toby did was give you an order, and you honored it wit'out question."

"So, what we're about to do is the real deal?"

"No bullshit."

"Damn," muttered Tootsie. "I'd always wanted to do some shit like this, after all the hell them bastards took me through these past ten years," she said.

"Well, here's your chance, boo."

"Cool."

When Toby exited the sports bar on Tennessee Street, and got back in the car, she pulled out a piece of paper and a photo, and handed it over to Tootsie.

"That's your man right here, Toot. Study him and learn his habits, and be ready to execute, when the time comes."

Sheena gave Tootsie that look and smirked mischievously.

"Consider it done, Toby. I won't let you down. That's what I came all the way down here from Chicago for," Tootsie replied, before hitting the blunt. "To prove my worth and stand for something…You know what I mean?"

"I have great faith in you," said Toby.

"Thank you."

From there, the trio rode out and vibed with one another, as the evening carried on, with other activities. Toby wanted to make sure that her last two recruits were on point and familiar with the area. She did not wat to make the same mistakes Skarr did, with her recruits. That's why Toby was adamant about keeping them close, and preparing them for the mission that was about to take place. The plan was near now. It was almost that time to execute, but still, in the back of her mind, Toby was still concerned about Kiara and her situation. She would focus on the plan ahead, first. Once that plan succeeded, she would then act upon the choice she'd already made. It wasn't long before Kiara would regain her freedom, and that's all that mattered at that moment. Freedom. To be set free. To stand against the odds and never fold.

Chapter 14

In their hands were *"Get Well"* balloons, teddy bears, and shiny glittered cards, as they approached the room. Both Sassy and Stacy looked at one another in silent reproof of the two Royals posted up outside the door. They were Dejah's two best friends, both of whom Heaven had grown to love and adore over the years. Sassy especially, who was the light at the end of the tunnel for Heaven, numerous times. It was her and Stacy's fear of being caught up in what was going on around Heaven that took them this long to make their presence known. One had to be extremely careful, when there was a war going on in their midst.

When the two women made it to the door, one of the two Royals put up a hand to stop them. Both of them knew who the two Royals were and were quite cantankerous about their actions. Stacy stepped forward and attempted to move around them, to get to the door. When Blanca, one of the Royals, stiff-armed her, Stacy politely set down what she had in her hands on the floor. Then she was about to get in that bitch's chest, but was prevented from doing so, when the door opened and LaVetra stood there, looking out at them.

"No fussin," said the old lady, who was Marlon's aunt and another solid foundation of the family. "You may come inside, but leave that attitude at the door. Do I make myself clear?" she said testily.

Sassy nodded.

"Yes ma'am," said Stacy.

They entered the room, and looked for space around the room to put the balloons and stuff. There was so much more *"Get Well"* merchandise in the room that it was hard to find space, without it being in the way.

Also present in the room was Monica, who appeared to look worse for wear, two men that were unfamiliar to them, Aliyah Renee, Anya and Malik, and of course Ella Mae, who was busy knitting and humming softly to herself. It was so peaceful in the air, despite the pressure of Heaven lying in the bed, still clinging to life. Overall, there was a peaceful atmosphere that could not be denied, and that was a godsend, compared to the troubles beyond the other side of the door.

"How's my baby girl?" said Sassy, walking up to Heaven's bedside and leaning in to place a kiss upon her cheek. At the foot of the bed, Aliyah Renee lay asleep and snoring lightly.

"It's just a waiting game," said Anya, opening up a pack of animal crackers for her son. "But she's still healthy, and strong as an ox.

"But it's been two weeks, though," said Stacy.

Monica could only nod her head quietly. She was so filled with anguish and distress that it left her speechless. Having Heaven down and out in a coma was depressing.

"Some could last months, or a year, if they're lucky, but with Heaven's stubbornness and willpower, she stood a chance of regaining consciousness sooner than later," said the white guy sitting down next to Anya.

"And who the hell are you?" Sassy replied.

"Sassy!" Ella Mae glared in her direction, and Sassy clamped her lips shut.

Stacy elbowed her friend in the side and turned her gaze in the white man's direction, before kindly asking who the hell he was, as well.

"I'm sorry." He stood up swiftly. "I'm Professor Norris Briggs, from Florida State University, where Heaven was attending her classes, before her unfortunate incident." He extended his hand toward Sassy, and she took it, reluctantly. "Nice to meet you, Sassy," he smirked.

"And you are?" Stacy acknowledged the second guy occupying the room after the introductions with Norris.

Before he could introduce himself, the door opened and in walked Levi, once again. The last time he shown up there, he had come with some outrageous news, regarding Heaven and the abduction of federal Judge Magdalena Harrington's daughter. It was said that the abduction would be blamed on Royal Mafia, if Royal Mafia didn't cooperate in providing information that was needed to help the government officials locate the girl. The Royals claimed they had nothing to do with that.

"Here we go again wit' the bullshit," muttered Monica, when Levi walked through the door.

"What now?" Ella Mae grunted.

"Got some good news and some bad news," said Levi, dressed in his usual casual attire.

When Sassy and Stacy looked at him, they both frowned upon his existence. They knew exactly who he was, and didn't think too kindly of him being in their presence.

"The hook is off with the kidnapping incident, and your people are cleared on that matter," he said.

"So, they got the ones who did it?"

He shook his head no to Anya. "They got a good lead that doesn't have any relation to Royal Mafia," Levi said. "Frankly, that's a whole nother ball game that's..."

"That's out of their league? Is that what you were about to say, Levi?" said Monica.

Levi opened his mouth to respond, just as the door exploded inwardly and several FBI agents rushed into the room. Without so much as an ounce of mercy, two of the agents took ahold of Levi and slammed him, face first, into the floor. His teeth cracked and his nose bone shattered upon impact, as he was cuffed behind his back.

"What's the meaning of this?" Norris yelled in an outrage, as he watched the brutality before him. "There's children present, and you're being totally out of line here!"

"Out of line, ya say?" said the lead FBI agent, wearing the lettered windbreaker and a hardened expression. "You should've told that to this guy, before he decided to share critical federal government information with civilians."

"He's not FBI," said Monica.

"My point exactly."

"But apparently he got his critical federal government information from somewhere in your bureau, sir. If it's that critical, then you need to look in-house for the real perpetrator. Now would you please leave this room and allow this family to continue their grieving period," said Norris to the agent.

"So, you're the spokesperson for this family now, Briggs?"

"So, you know who I am?"

The bigger man's piercing gaze bore into Norris, as his men led Levi out of the room.

"I know you, Briggs, but your influence doesn't carry enough weight with my bureau, like your pop's once did," said the FBI agent.

"I stand on my own reputation, not my father's."

"Good day, Briggs," smirked the agent, before turning on his heels and making an exit.

When Norris decided to go after him, the other guy took him by the arm to keep him at bay. You could see the fire in his light blue eyes, and apparently, he wasn't just your average college professor.

"What was that all about?" asked LaVetra, now pulling the little girl up into her embrace, just to calm her nerves from being startled out of her sleep just now.

"That shit sounded personal," Anya replied.

"It sure did," added Ella Mae.

"That's because it is personal," said Norris Briggs.

Then he went on and admitted that his father was found dead in his home office a decade ago. Norman Briggs had been a very powerful man and in great health, prior to his demise, but it didn't take a genius to read between the lines of what Norris was really trying to say. His father's death was not by natural causes, but by the unseen hands of an enemy. That enemy was the FBI.

Chapter 15

Another week later, Dejah got the text message from Delani that the plan was going down tomorrow. She told Shoo Baby and Mookie what was about to transpire, and she wanted to make sure they were on one accord.

"Bring Jill in here for a minute, Shoo Baby," said Dejah, while sitting Indian style on her bottom bunk, ripping up old letters and cards and such. There was a pile of shredded paper on the bed in front of her.

Shoo Baby left the cell without question.

It was just after that noon hour count time, and the doors had just opened to release the inmates. Any minute, there would be movement for lunch. They had enough food in their canteen, and enough product to buy whatever other food they desired and didn't have. A few minutes later, Jill entered the room, eating a glazed honeybun from the vending machine. She was a thirty year old female, serving a five year bid for keeping it real with her nigga, who wasn't keeping it real with her. Jill was dark chocolate complexion, with bowlegs, and fearless as all get out. She was originally from Panama City, Florida, but had gotten cased up down in Tampa. It didn't matter where she was at, Jill was the type of bitch who would adjust to any environment she found herself in. She was one of the few standup bitches in the building, and that's why Dejah had sent for her.

"What're you doing, some spring cleaning or something?" said Jill with a smirk on her face.

"Sit down right there at the foot of the bunk," Dejah told her, with a humbled gesture.

Mookie was busily doing her own thing, tying up a few loose ends herself (meaning saying goodbye to her little girlfriend she had been kicking it with lately).

"What's up, Dej?" Jill had taken her seat as instructed, and tried not to drop crumbs onto the bunk.

"You know I respect you, Jill. You're not like all the rest of them bitches out there. You stand for what's right, and don't mind getting your hands dirty to protect your honor."

"Can't be too careful on this shit, Dej."

Dejah nodded. "Trust me, I know, but my time here is about to expire, my love," she said.

That made Jill's eyes pop out with astonishment. "They gave you some time already?" she asked.

"No."

Jill paused. "No?"

Right then, Dejah reached behind her back and brought forth a box of chocolate Nutty Buddy wafers. She offered the box to Jill, and she took it into her possession.

"It's five ounces of K2, Molly, and loose cigarettes in there, Jill. Make use of it to the best of your ability," said Dejah. She watched as Jill's mouth dropped. "I trust you to take care of your business, and not let the small shit get to you."

"And please take care of Vera Mae for me," said Shoo Baby, who had been leaning against the door jamb the whole time. She had mad love for the old lady.

"You know I will," said Jill.

"Jill," Dejah regained her attention. "Do your time and go home. Fuck that no good nigga, live your life the way you wanna live it now. The streets don't owe you shit, and neither do his ass, Jill. Don't be no fool. Your youth was stolen by that fool, and now your freedom. What more do you need to lose for you to see that you are special and blessed beyond the dreams of a million other women?"

"Your worth is priceless," said Shoo Baby.

Then Dejah hugged the other woman and assured her that she would keep in touch with her.

"And Jill," Dejah stopped her at the door, just before she made her exit. "Don't mention any of this to nobody," she said. "It's very detrimental that you keep this shit under lock and key, until after we're gone.

Jill said, "What's understood don't need to be explained, Dej. I gotcha, big sista. No doubt."

Shoo Baby bumped fists with her as she finally took her leave from the room.

After Jill left the room, Shoo Baby went over and sat down across from Dejah. For a long moment, she just sat there watching as she resumed tearing up paper. She was making sure that she left no traces of information behind, after she was gone, nothing that the Feds didn't already know, for that matter.

Dejah was banking everything on this plan that Delani had been brewing for weeks. To him, the mission was ready to execute, and he had no worries. He had given their outside team a week in advance to make sure that all their positions were confirmed because one mistake could cost them their lives and their freedom. But overall, the Hooliganz Crime Gang were focused and ready to move, and by any means necessary, they were going to succeed. They were about to create history. The whole world was about to know their name.

"Where is Mook?" asked Dejah.

"You know where Mookie is, Dej," Shoo Baby said in a matter of fact way, obviously irritated by the subject matter.

"Upstairs wit' you-know-who?"

"Daisy."

Dejah nodded. "Her."

Shoo Baby let out an exasperated breath. "The last thang we need is for her to be caught up in her feelings over a bitch right now, and this the last motherfucker I woulda ever expected to get down like that," she said.

"Love moves in mysterious ways, Baby."

"Love," Shoo Baby grunted. "It's prolly your ass, the reason our girl is swinging from another bitch clit!"

"Don't blame me," said Dejah.

"Whateva. I just hope she ain't up there running her damn mouth about the wrong thangs."

That statement made Dejah pause and look up at her, with a very sharp glare in her eyes.

"I'm just saying, Dej," Shoo Baby spoke up again. "We both know how talkative Mook can be at times."

"Mookie knows better than to run her mouth about that," said Dejah, with a stern expression on her face.

"Run my mouth about what," said Mookie.

Both Dejah and Shoo Baby looked up to see Mookie entering the room. She wore a very expressionless face, but you could easily see the sadness in her eyes. Dejah was bothered by this, yet she didn't wanna put her girl on the spot like that. But when the doors closed again, she most definitely was gonna check her about wearing her emotions on her sleeve. Some may see that as a sign of weakness, and weakness could get you murdered.

"You up there all boo'd up and shit, and we was hoping you wasn't up there running your damn mouth," said Shoo Baby.

"Now why would I do that?" she asked.

"Why would you want to wait until now to fuck around wit' bitches? What about JoJo? And of course, Bryshon, wit' his aggravating ass?" Shoo baby said.

Mookie just glared at her, as if she wanted some smoke.

"Y'all dead that shit," said Dejah.

"Yeah, a'ight." Shoo Baby stood up and moved towards Mookie to come face to face with her. "Just so that you know, Mookie, I will step on that bitch up there, if she even looks like she knows something," she sneered.

"She doesn't. And since we're at it, Shoo Baby, you got one more time to question my loyalty, and I'm gon' make you catch a fade."

"That's how you feel?"

"That's what it is, Shoo Baby."

"Then we can get down right now," Shoo Baby said, as Dejah hurriedly jumped to her feet and moved in between the two women.

"The fuck is wrong wit' y'all? I mean, for real, for real," snapped Dejah, looking from one to the other, and sensing the tension there. "Is there something I need to know about? Shoo Baby? Mook?" She knew if she didn't do anything, then all hell was gonna break loose up in there.

Something was happening between the two women.

"Mookie?" Dejah laid a hand upon her shoulder.

With the suck of her teeth, Shoo Baby brushed past them, while bumping shoulders with Mookie on purpose. She then walked out the room, without another word. When Mookie stared after her, as though contemplating going after Shoo Baby, she was immediately brought back around to Dejah. Dejah then took her by the hand and pulled her over to the bunk to sit her down.

"What's going on wit' y'all?" asked Dejah.

"She's jealous, Dej, that's all." Mookie nodded evenly. "Yeah ever since she learned that Toby stole her little boyfriend, she been in her feelings. Now that she sees me doing my thang wit' Daisy, she want to get all salty and shit."

"Wait as sec," said Dejah. "Who the hell Toby supposed to stole from her?"

"Ty," Mook replied.

"White Boy Ty? Our Ty?"

Mookie nodded.

A shocked expression appeared on Dejah's face. She had not known of this at all. She had no clue Shoo Baby had been messing with White Boy Ty, nor was she aware of the relationship between him and Toby. To Dejah, that was an unexpected thing to do and one helluva force to be reckoned with together. Now Dejah knew for a fact that a beef could spark between Shoo Baby and Toby, which was another thing that could turn everything upside down for the team. That's what Dejah feared. Battles of the heart were a dangerous game, even deadly, and somebody just might die behind this.

Chapter 16

At that same hour, Kwame Dawson was sitting behind his large mahogany desk, when there was a knock at the door. He looked up from what he was reading in a file folder lain flat upon his desk. He stared towards the door, and told whoever it was to come in. The door opened and in peeped Lynn Coben, the matured Caucasian secretary.

"Um, you have two potential clients, but they do not have an appointment, sir," said Lynn.

Kwame wasn't the type to neglect potential customers.

"Is it another couple?" he asked.

Couples were very particular with what kind of house they were interested in buying, especially if there were kids involved, like the last round. They spent restless hours searching for the perfect house.

"Yes, sir," she said. "They are indeed."

With a sigh, he said, "Send them, Lynn."

After Lynn ducked back outside the door, Kwame bookmarked the file he was reading and shut it. A minute later the door was opened and in walked the last two people Kwame expected to see.

"Thank you, Lynn."

Kwame rose up to his feet behind the desk and waited until his secretary closed the door. Then he turned his gaze back on Rikah and Vontay and said, "What a surprise. So what do I owe this visit?"

Rikah stepped forward as she clutched the handle of the large duffel bag and dropped it on top of the desk. Then Vontay did the same with the bag in his hand as well.

"We came to look for houses," said Rikah.

"You said houses, as in plural," he replied, surprised.

"My grammar is superb, Kwame, so there's no need for me to emphasize my point further than what's in those two bags," said Rikah, with an elaborate gesture towards the desk.

Kwame looked down at the two duffel bags and automatically knew what was inside, but he still couldn't shake the fact that, not too long ago, he'd watched Rikah murder four people in front of him, and kidnap his brother's daughter. The very same person whom he had attempted to kill after she had spared his life, on that very same night. Now here she was, thousands of miles away from home, on his territory, seeking help. Kwame didn't quite know what to make of this matter and almost found himself speechless. He couldn't help but to assume some trickery was in play. He opened one of the bags and was granted the sight of cold hard cash inside.

"How much in total?" asked Kwame, feeling himself beginning to perspire from his anxiety.

"A total of 3.2 million," said Rikah.

"And you're interested in multiple residences?"

She gave him a testy look.

Something was going on and Kwame knew it to be very serious for them to have come this long way. Whatever it was, Rikah was to be ensured that her and her people had secured shelter when needed.

"And what's the timetable?"

"By tomorrow," said Vontay.

"Tomorrow?"

Rikah said, "Time is of essence."

Of course, he wanted to decline and just send them on their way, but for them to be there meant that they knew more about his personal life than he cared to believe. Refusing them, at that moment, could also place his family at risk, and Hooliganz Crime Gang was the last ones he would want on his bad side, especially now, after what all they'd been through together.

"Rikah, this is my business, and it's legit. I don't want no trouble. I will give you what you ask, but all I ask of you is to…" Kwame was saying, before being cut off.

"Protect your honor and your family, right?"

He didn't reply.

"I know exactly what's going on here, Kwame. Trust me, I wouldn't have come here, if I didn't believe that you could help us. I just brought you 3.2 million dollars in cash. Help us help you, and I guarantee you won't be sorry," said Rikah."

"That's easier said than done," he reluctantly said.

"Can we go see some houses now?"

"We can," he replied. "But not here, in New Jersey."

"Where then?"

"I can situate you in New York, instead," Kwame replied.

"That's even better for us," said Vontay.

Rikah nodded agreeably.

The HCG crew was coming to New York, and Kwame didn't know whether he should be scared or upset about that. He would do his part, though, and not only because of the large amount of money involved, but because he knew Jamir would be involved. Jamir was his estranged nephew, his twin brother's son. His devotion to his family was why he was totally doing it. Kwame was very family oriented, and loyal to a fault. So he made the trip to New York, where his real estate company branched to, from New Jersey. He wanted them far away as possible from his family. He had a wife and two daughters to protect, and that's all that mattered.

Meanwhile, Rikah had told him, in so many words, that something was about to go down and their place of residences needed to be ready, without failure. They couldn't afford complications, at that point. The stakes were too high.

By that evening, Kwame had done his part and Rikah was gratified with the results. She immediately called home and told Jamir what was to be expected.

Later that night, Kwame lay in bed with his wife, Daphney, of twenty-two years, quiet and very disturbed by what he now knew was coming. He didn't want to be involved, but was left with no other choice.

Daphney rolled over on her side to look at him. He was just lying there, staring up at the ceiling, with his hands behind his head. He hadn't moved from that position in more than an hour.

"I can feel it, ya know?" she whispered, before laying a hand upon his bare chest. "You're worried about something."

"It's just some stuff," he replied.

"I think it's deeper than that, Kwame." Daphney was a dedicated psychologist, who worked at the local children's psychiatric hospital for a living. "So, let's not start with your avoiding my concern because you're concerned about my feelings.

"It's still nothing I can't rectify, on my own."

"And yet you are still avoiding the issue."

That's when Kwame reached over and gathered his loving wife into his arms. He then kissed the top of her head and said, "Don't fret, baby, I got it under control. I love you. Now get some sleep, Dalph. You have a long day tomorrow."

"I should be telling you the same thing," she murmured, and then gave up trying to get through to him. Daphney knew whatever it was dominating her husband's thought process, it was weighing on his emotional state as well. Kwame was more than just worried about work. He was scared. Terrified.

Chapter 17

The following night, a black Lexus SUV and matching colored Cadillac Escalade truck turned onto Jasper Road and came to a parallel halt, right next to one another. Both driver and front passenger window went down to reveal Toby and Lil Eddie, sitting across from one another.

"Y'all ready?"

"You know we is, Toby. Let's do the damn thang," said Lil Eddie, with a firm salute. Between both vehicles, there were ten of them in all, and they were war ready. It was going down tonight. Shit was about to get real critical in the field.

"No pressure," said Toby.

"No pressure."

Then both vehicles sprang forward. Moments later, they came to rest outside a big, white house. The doors to both SUV's opened and eight Hooliganz jumped out at once. Four hurried towards the front door of the house, while the other four fanned out along the property with guns at the ready. There was nothing less than thirty rounds equipped in their artillery, and extra ammunition when needed. From bullet proof vest to military formation, the Hooliganz were strategically active and fearless as they come.

They had come for Warden William McCulley, who would be the star character of the night. He was the key player, the main attraction, the golden boy with all the power. When the team of Hooliganz forced themselves through the front door, they entered the home like the SWAT Team.

Warden McCulley was occupying the kitchen with his wife, assisting her with the dishes. When they heard the front door being kicked in, McCulley instantly reached for a butcher knife from the cutting board.

"Stay behind me," said McCulley to his wife, when the first Hooligan stepped through the door of kitchen.

It was Jamir, who was behind the mask, with the AK-47 in his hand. He ignored the knife, flipped the stock of the assault rifle, and bashed him right between the eyes with it. All McCulley saw was the flash of a bright light, before everything went dark.

"Take him out to the truck and collect the rest of the family," ordered Jamir, and two Hooliganz took ahold of the big man to carry him outside.

"Please don't hurt my children," cried the wife.

Jamir stepped forward. "That is only determined by whether your husband cooperate wit' us or not," he told her.

"He will," she said fearfully. "He will, for the sake of his family."

"And so would you, too," said Jamir.

She was snatched up next, along with her two teenage sons, and told to keep extremely quiet or they would die. Then they were taken outside and loaded into a waiting minivan at the curb out front. They did not make a sound whatsoever.

During that very minute, twenty-six other Hooliganz were creating the same strategy to other government officials, who worked under the Warden's authority. From the assistant warden of the federal holding facility, all the way down to the current officer in charge of the prison. Every higher up official with general authority over the night shift, their families were targeted and taken, just as the warden's.

Delani had thought back on the plan of attack that Lyonell had used against the Gutter Boyz Movement, when Killa Don and his whole team had gotten slaughtered, along with dozens of the crew members, all at the same time. That was the move tonight, but no one was dying unless it was deemed necessary.

On the way to the prison, Warden McCulley was awakened and given instructions on what needed to be done. If he so much as hesitated to follow through, not only would his family die, but he and his colleagues, as well. The big man did not care about the repercussions afterwards, all he cared about was the safety of his dear family. So, he agreed to do as he was instructed, and then he was dropped off outside the federal detention facility building.

By this time, the rest of the shift officials were alerted of the situation and waiting on his arrival. When he finally stepped foot in the building, he barked out orders to have all members of the HCG brought up front to the administration building. No one dared to question his authority because they already knew what was at stake. One false move and their whole families would be dead.

When Delani heard his cell door groan open, he was already ready to make his move, and so was LJ, Shamar, Booby, Kahlil, Dejah, and the rest of the crew. It was happening, and all they could think about was how close to their freedom they were with every following step they took.

As this was going on, all the other inmates and the lower officials could only watch, with shocked looks on their faces. Even Big Los McClendon and a few of his homies were being set free, as well. Delani promised him that it would happen and now he was owning up to that promise.

Warden McCulley already had the entrance gate to the prison opened and welcoming. He stood right there, along with several of his men, holding the gate and watching with closed-mouth contempt as the Hooliganz Crime Gang was set free at last. A fleet of vehicles were waiting anxiously for their arrival, and when that moment came, they all got into their motorcade and got ghost. They sped away from the scene in a parade of vehicles and thudding hearts of joy. Adrenaline rushed through them, like a dose of morphine.

The mission was far from complete, though, because they needed to get as far away as possible from the devastation they'd created. Going back home was a total no-no now, too risky to chance, so straight on the interstate they went, heading north, and not stopping for nothing or no one. The moment they crossed over the Florida-Georgia line, they all allowed themselves a grateful breath of relief, but they still had a long road ahead of them, and had to be ready for any inconveniences.

Delani was humbled as a monk, as he sat back and stared out the side window into the night. He was crying inside, but he refused to let it show. His team had done the unthinkable. What was so overwhelming about the whole thing, no one died in the process of the great escape. It was mission accomplished. From behind his brother's seat, Jamir reached around and hugged Delani, just like that.

"We did it, Dee. Now we change the game from here," he said.

"The game is already changed, little bro. This is just the next level," said Delani.

An hour later, Delani ordered the motorcade to stop somewhere in the neck of the woods of Albany, Georgia. There they stopped at a secluded location that Jamir had pointed out from memory of visiting the area several times already. The location was the old bumpy road, leading up to an old hangar building, which sat out in the open.

"What's going on?" asked Toby.

"I want everybody outside to witness this," said Delani, who then took the .50 caliber pistol from Kweli.

Dejah and Rikah were holding hands, as Mookie and Zamon stood next to one another. Moments later, all but the Hooliganz who were tying up the few loose ends were present. Even Big Los and several of his men were in the midst.

"I'm not gon' even make this shit a speech because we got shit to do, but you all are familiar wit' the price of disloyalty, right?" said Delani.

Some answered and some just looked at each other, because it was clear that Delani was directing this subject matter to someone in particular. Without further ado, Delani walked right up to Kahlil and shot him dead in the face. Then he stood over his cousin's twitching body and filled it up with more hot lead. In the process, Dejah told everybody the reason Kahlil lost his life tonight.

"He sold us out?" White Boy Ty said in disbelief, as he stood staring down at Kahlil's dead body.

"Make this your final warning for any of y'all who dare to cross out the Hooliganz Crime Gang. Now let's go," Delani said, and made his way back to his SUV.

Everybody else followed suit.

"He's back," whispered Toby.

Sure enough, Delani was back indeed. He was the heart of the organization. He was HCG and now the whole world would know.

Chapter 18

Harold and Kiara were sound asleep in their home, when they were awakened by the sound of the new iPhone Toby had given them vibrating on the nightstand. Kiara looked at the irritating phone and saw that its time read 8:39 in the morning. Initially, she was aggravated, but when she picked up the ringing phone and saw that it was a blocked number, that intensified her annoyance.

"Hello?" she answered with a yawn.

"I love you, beautiful lady."

"Delani?"

"I did it, Mama. It's done."

"Huh?" Kiara sat up farther in the bed, as Harold turned over to look at her questioningly.

"It's our son," she told her husband. "Good morning, sweetie. How are you?"

"Turn on the news, Mama," he said.

She nudged her husband and told him to grab the remote control to turn on the TV. Harold did as he was told, but in a groggy manner, as he threw his well-muscled legs over the side of the bed.

"Oh. My. God," gasped Kiara the instant she saw what she was viewing on WCTV news. Plastered on the screen were mugshots of every member of the Hooliganz Crime Gang that escaped from the federal detention holding facility the night before.

"He really did it," swallowed Harold nervously.

As the news reporter explained the actions taken to achieve the great escape, silent tears of joy welled up in Kiara's brown eyes.

"Nobody got hurt. Thank you, Lord," she said.

"That's the beauty of it, Mama."

Right then the news commentator described the escape as being one of the cleverest and most committed acts in history. Hooliganz Crime Gang and its accomplices were now considered armed and dangerous, and seemed to have vanished without a trace.

No sooner than Kiara and Harold disconnected with Delani, after he assured them that he was safe, the FBI came knocking on their front door. When answered, a team of tactical gear wearing FBI agents boisterously forced themselves inside the house. Of course, Kiara and Harold were already prepared for their presence, and just let them do what they came to do.

"We're looking for your son, Delani" said Agent Thomas Lowell. "He's a wanted fugitive to our bureau."

"That we can see," retorted Kiara. "Just tell your guys to be careful wit' my stuff and don't break."

The instant the word came out of her mouth she heard the sound of something breaking down the hall. When his wife took off in that direction Harold stepped up and confronted Agent Lowell.

"You are not gonna find my son here, sir, so you are wastin' your time."

"Am I?" Lowell replied.

"It's obvious, isn't it? To pull a stunt like that to escape from your custody, you really think he would risk all that by coming here? You can't be that stupid," said Harold, as he stood toe to toe with the agent.

"Indeed, you have a point," said Agent Lowell. "But I've seen stranger things happen during my time with the bureau."

"You won't see it here," said Harold.

"Sure, I'm not."

A minute later, Agent Lowell was approached by one of his secondary lead men. When he was told the house was clear, Harold read something between the two men that he immediately thought was suspicious.

"Okay guys, let's head out." Agent Lowell headed for the front door, without another word to Harold. He and his team exited from the house back into their vehicles, screeching from the scene.

After they left, Harold went in search of his wife, and found her inside of Delani's old bedroom.

"What's wrong? He replied.

When Kiara spun around, Harold saw that she was holding a large picture frame, pressed against her breast. He stepped closer and laid a hand upon her arm.

"Look at them, Harold. Look how innocent they all look in here."

Kiara showed her husband the photo of the twins, Heaven, Jamir, and Shamar, when they were just little children. The photo was of them standing out in the front yard on the twins' tenth birthday.

"Mischievous as hell, yeah," said Harold.

"You remember this day, Harold?"

"How can I not?" he chuckled. "Vermani snuck his bad ass in our liquor cabinet and drank that bottle of E&J, until he was throwin' up and shittin' all over himself."

"And you made me clean it." Kiara punched him in the arm.

"You wanted to," he said. "You said it."

"No the hell I didn't, Harold. Uh-uh." She shook her head.

A momentary silence ensued between them.

"Kiara? Harold? Y'all in here?" came the sound of LaShonda's voice, calling from up front.

When they answered, and told her where they were, LaShonda appeared in the bedroom doorway, moments later.

"Got y'all too, huh?"

"A waste of damn time," said Kiara.

"Y'all know while they were in here…"

Harold stopped LaShonda from continuing, by placing his hand over her mouth. He shook his head no to her and gave her the shush sound.

Kiara said, "What is it?"

"Just start packing everything you don't want destroyed in the house, Kay," he replied cautiously.

"Destroyed? For what? What are you talkin' about?"

Harold whispered in her ear that the whole house was bugged with listening devices and hidden video cameras, planted by the FBI. He told them about his suspicion between Agent Lowell and one of his men communicating earlier. LaShonda admitted that she had actually caught one of the men in the act of planting a device beneath the flat screen Sony TV in her living room. She didn't say anything, and just played dumb, like she didn't know what was going on.

"I'm about to burn the house down," said Harold, and got a weird look from his wife.

"Burn down the house? My house?"

Harold nodded, and Kiara slapped the taste out of his mouth.

"Are you outta your goddam mind, Harold?"

"Not when your dream house is already situated, my love. I said what I said. I'm burning it down. No exceptions." Harold then turned around and walked away from his wife and through the door, without a backwards glance.

At his exit, Kiara looked at LaShonda, speechless and totally dismayed by what was just delivered to her by Harold.

"Your husband wants a new start," said LaShonda.

"But this is our home," whined Kiara.

"And all it is now is a reminder of what used to be, Kay. Harold wants a better life for you two. Your future together and your happiness is what matters most, right now. So let your man do his job, and be grateful that you still go one to be there for you," said LaShonda, and then she left the room next.

"It's time for all of us to make a change for the better," sang LaShonda, as she made her way back through the house.

All Kiara could do was shake her head. "Can't believe this nigga's bout to burn my damn house down."

Chapter 19

Over the course of the next two and a half weeks, there were no sightings of Delani and his now notorious HCG crew. It was as though they all had fallen off the face of the earth. Meanwhile, Baiyina and LeLe were down to a total of ten loyal Royals who didn't abandon ship. When Skarr went around trying to recruit more Royals, no one wanted to have parts of the crew, if it wasn't by Heaven or Toby's pickings. Nobody wanted to have dealings with Baiyina, whose life was now hanging in the balance, where the other Royals devoted to Toby and Heaven was concerned.

Baiyina was seeing it clearly, she wasn't fit to rule, and that was giving Royal Mafia a black eye. With Hooliganz Crime Gang back in the streets, and with Delani resuming his leadership over the crew, that was something to definitely worry about. Baiyina feared that if her former Royals didn't try to knock her off first, Delani, no doubt, would get the job done, especially now, after Kahlil's body had been found. Baiyina knew his death was caused by none other than his very own cousin. There was a matter of time before Delani showed his face, and when he did, it wouldn't be pretty. When it happened, somebody was going to die in the process. That nigga was a monster.

When Baiyina reached the intersection of Appleyard Drive and Capitol Circle, she brought her Maserati to a stop at the red light, and looked towards Club Epic's direction, to her left. It was Freaky Friday, and the line outside was around the corner, when she pulled up on the scene. The traffic light turned green, and she veered left onto Pensacola Street. Her cellphone buzzed inside her front pocket, interrupting her thoughts on what Skarr had told her earlier. She retrieved the phone and saw that the caller was her new reliable contact.

"What is it, Spencer? Talk to me, and I'll talk back," Baiyina replied in her smooth demeanor.

"I'm calling wit' information you asked me about. According to my sources, Orlando Sanchez, a.k.a. Oso, is a well-known Mexican Cartel affiliate, and of high rank. He is said to be currently present at the Four Seasons on Broadway, and he has been here for the past two days, in anticipation of attending his niece's graduation," said Spencer Proctor.

"Good. Good," Baiyina anxiously replied. "I need the room number he's staying in. Do you have his direct location?"

"Affirmative."

"Text me the information, Spencer."

"Consider it done. Now where's my money you promised?" he asked.

Baiyina checked him aggressively about questioning her, and told him he would have his money once she had dealt with Oso Sanchez accordingly. After disconnecting with Spencer, she laid the phone down on the passenger seat and continued driving down Pensacola Street. Up ahead, she noticed blue and red lights flashing, and automatically assumed there had been a traffic accident or something, but just as soon as she laid eyes on the black BMW in the middle of the intersection, her heart suddenly squeezed with panic.

"That better not be one of mines," she muttered to herself, as she turned into the entrance of a Subway restaurant across the street.

There were at least a dozen Royals, who owned that model of car, thanks to Heaven having gifted them all one each, as a token of commitment. Seeing this particular BMW now raised alarm bells in her head. As Baiyina exited her car, a minute later, and fixed her gaze on the scene before her, she could see that authorities had both the driver and passenger doors open. She looked at the chrome rims and could only think of one person, who actually had those type on their car.

"LeLe," she gasped. "No!"

The way the crime scene investigators were moving around the car, there was no doubt that the occupants of the BMW were dead. Baiyina had been on her way to meet with LeLe, but now that didn't seem so likely. After a few seconds of watching the crime scene unit conduct their investigation, she returned back to her Maserati and refreshed her cup with Hennessy, for a drink. As Baiyina took a drink from the cup and relished the burn going down smoothly, the passenger door opened, and another body slid into the car beside her. That same instant there was a tap on the window to her left, and when Baiyina turned to look, she didn't like what she saw. It was NaiNai, and the person next to her was Tilly. A sudden wave of trepidation washed over her and brought on a cold shiver, running down her spine.

"The hell you got going on Tilly?" said Baiyina with an act of bravado, but it was lost on Tilly.

"It's time for you to step down, Bai."

"Step down?"

Tilly nodded. "Yep."

When Baiyina opened her mouth to respond, a sharp blade ran across her neck from ear to ear. Baiyina paused in astonishment. Then, when she realized what had just transpired, she reached her hand up to her throat, and felt the blood gushing from her opened wound.

"No. Why, Tilly?" Baiyina cried out, and tried to reach out towards Tilly.

Tilly punched her in the eye. "You don't deserve the throne, bitch," said Tilly, before she placed the silenced gun to Baiyina's head and sent two slugs to her brain.

While Baiyina lay slumped behind the wheel of her car, Tilly slid back out into the night.

"So, it's done?" asked Gucci.

She was hobbling towards Tilly, her injured leg still not fully healed yet. After the deaths of Tori and Diva that one fateful night at Uncle Bart's house, it was Tilly, whom she had called to rescue her. Since then, they had been plotting on a takeover to regain the respect that Heaven had built around their organization. A hug from Tilly was the only answer Gucci needed to know what was to happen next.

"Well, we got Skarr, too," said NaiNai walking up to them with three other Royals behind her. "What do you want us to do with her?" she asked.

"You wanna go have a look at Baiyina and rephrase what you just said NaiNai? Never mind." Tilly waved off the question and said, "Kill her. Every last one of them must die so that we can prevail again."

"Say no more."

"And what about LeLe?" asked Gucci.

"What about her?"

It wasn't LeLe, who was inside the BMW, surrounded by crime scene investigators. It was her no good baby daddy, Pitt, who had beat her almost to an inch of her life tonight. Luckily, Gucci and Tilly had arrived there on time to stop Pitt from actually killing her, but he got what he deserved, for his demise had been a long time coming. He and his brother, Mario, were delivered that fateful blow tonight, a penalty that was inevitable.

"We takin her back or what?"

Tilly gave Gucci's question a brief thought. "I'll think about it and let you know later, but for now, we gotta move," she said. "We gotta save what's left of Royal Mafia and make the streets great again."

"Spoken like a true Royal," smirked NaiNai.

Tilly smirked back at her. It was clean up time, time to reconstruct, and destroy everything else that stood in their path. Crazy how Toby was still calling the shots with the team members, but that's why Tilly was there to rectify things, when her cousin couldn't personally be there to do it herself. Revolution was in progress. No exceptions.

Chapter 20

It was 9:00 a.m. the following morning and Delani was watching the news. The headlines read, "Another night of vicious massacre in Florida's Capitol." It told the story of a female queenpin, by the name of Baiyina Givens, murdered brutally in a Subway parking lot. Her murder was followed by another series of murders of her own Royal Mafia members. Thirteen people were killed in relation to Baiyina's influence. It which was also assumed she had been eliminated due to a turf war.

"That's bullshit," said Shamar from over Delani's shoulder, behind the plush sofa. "How can it be a turf war when the only people dead are Royals?"

Delani cut the TV off. Toby was rolling up a blunt on the sofa next to him. Across from them sat White Boy Ty, who was scrolling through his new cellphone. The look he had on his face was one of focus. Delani appeared to be pissed off about something.

"That's because my cousin is doing everything I told her to do," said Toby.

"Which is?" Dejah entered the room next.

She looked well-rested and refreshed in her casual attire and sandals, and every time Shamar laid eyes on her, all he did was smile now. He was happy to have her back in his presence.

"Process of elimination," said Toby. "Tilly was already reassembling her own team of Royals, who were totally against the shit Baiyina was enforcing. So, I advised her to utilize her own authority and dismantle their whole operation."

"They dismantled it alright," chuckled White Boy Ty. "Now who is gonna be the next in line for Royal Mafia?"

"Who else?" Toby said.

"Tilly?"

Toby shrugged. "She'd earned her keep thus far."

The crew was laying low, out in Wilton Long Island, in a nice seven bedroom mansion that Kwame had leased out to them. The big house was of Polynesian-style with antique settings, from its antique wide pine floors to several chandeliers hanging about the high ceilings throughout the residence. The mansion reminded Dejah of her old house back home, before everything went south.

Some of the other crew members were spread out in Yonkers, Harlem, Queens, and even Brooklyn. Some laying low in their brownstones, condos, and townhouses, but only ventured out at nighttime, when needed. LJ wanted his own space, and was out in Harlem, maintaining his seclusion. He had a lot on his mind and didn't want to deal with many people. He was free physically, but yet still imprisoned within his own personal predicament. He felt if they had just been patient and waited a little while longer, that the Feds would have let them go, when they didn't have a solid enough case to hold them. Now he was a fugitive, on the run, and on top of that, he couldn't be with Heaven or his daughter because it would be too dangerous to do so. LJ felt like shit right now, but he would come along eventually. At least that's what Bizzy chose to believe.

Being a fugitive on the run was exhausting in a sense, and you always have to look over your shoulder. One misstep could bring the whole team crashing down.

"Any word from Rikah about that situation we talked about Dee?" asked Dejah.

She was missing Shoo Baby and Mookie's presence, after being stuck with them all that time at the federal building. Shoo Baby was feeling some type of way about Ty and Toby's relationship, and was trying to stay as far away from them as possible.

"I spoke wit' her early this morning," said Delani. The mission is still going through.

"And you sure this shit gon' work?"

"And what mission is this exactly?" asked Toby. She had fired up the blunt and passed it to Delani.

"While we're up here hidin' out, I thought we need a reliable resource of authority that'll be useful to the team. Remember a few days ago on the news, where a woman and her two little sons were kidnapped?" said Delani.

"The wife of a police detective," Toby replied.

Bizzy and White Boy Ty looked at each other knowingly, but not of the actual situation itself.

"That was Rikah's work," said Delani.

"What?" Toby froze in amazement. "I mean, why? Why Dee?"

"Kidnappin' up here is almost normal, compared to some other places. But it's not common that the family of a cop is kidnapped, especially one who's a decorated detective and wit' a shitload of enemies he'd crossed. What we doing is taking his family, letting him suffer for a while, and in the process, we find out which one of his enemies is motivated enough to do it," said Delani before Toby cut in.

"Then put it on them, by contactin' the detective wit' the information, in exchange for his loyalty to us."

"But how are we gonna make the contact?" She asked.

"I got that part already under control, my nigga."

"How?" Toby persisted.

"Through Sonya."

"Who the fuck is Sonya?"

That's when Dejah spoke up. "She is the crackhead bitch over in Harlem that Wank Wank took under his wing. She knows what's going on in the streets of New York, and has been a lot of help, since we arrived."

"So that's the plan, okay."

Toby nodded and got up to walk over to where White Boy Ty was sitting. She pulled him up to his feet, and said, "Walk out back wit' me, Ty."

After they left, Shamar leapt over the back of the sofa and landed in the seat beside Delani. Delani looked over at him like he was crazy.

"Any word on Hev?"

"Nope," Shamar answered grudgingly.

Dejah said, "Don't you think it's time that you tell LJ about baby girl, Shamar?"

He looked over at her quietly.

Delani said, "The longer you take to tell him the truth, the worse the situation gon' get when you do, if you do."

"In my own time," said Shamar.

"When the fuck is your own time, bro?"

When Delani had recently learned that Aliyah Renee is Shamar's biological daughter, he was mad as hell. He felt crossed a little bit, by their secrecy, and now, as Dejah brought the matter back up, he was really anxious to hear what Shamar had to say.

"LJ's gonna lose his mind over that shit," said Dejah.

"And Shamar might have to kill him, too," said Delani, as he held Dejah's gaze. Then he hit the blunt again, before passing it over to Shamar.

Shamar still didn't say a word further.

"However you gotta do it, brah, handle that shit so you can get it past you," added Delani.

After a few pulls from the blunt, Shamar passed it back to Delani, and got up and left the room. He was obviously battling with his own conscience over the situation. Delani didn't even bother to press the issue.

"He's gonna kill LJ," muttered Delani. "How much you wanna bet, he gonna take brah all the way up through there?"

"I'm not bettin' on that shit, Dee."

"Shamar knows that's the only way to go about it because LJ damn sure ain't gon' be humble about it."

Dejah just shook her head sadly.

"Shamar ain't gon' play with his ass. Watch and see. LJ gon' make brah kill him. Watch."

Delani already knew why Shamar was so hesitant to respond, where the situation between him and LJ was concerned. Shamar didn't want to think about killing LJ because he knew how much that would affect Heaven. Hurting Heaven was the last thing any one of them wanted to do. But if LJ found out the truth about baby girl, not only would he be crushed, but would have blood in his eyes, too. He was already going through it, now that he couldn't be there for his baby girl and Heaven. The truth would only add fuel to the fire. It was going to get ugly. Matters like that couldn't wait too long before it exploded in all their faces, on its own. It was a wonder LJ did not see the resemblance of Shamar in Aliyah. That child looked exactly like him. The more the truth was prolonged, the clearer it would be revealed during Aliyah's development. Situations like that had killed many men. Somebody had to die, but who?

Chapter 21

It wasn't until yesterday that Jamir and several of his team members returned home, after their long stint of laying low and unseen. Prior to doing so, Jamir and his crew had already established a credible alibi, with credible people, whose word would be challenged but found substantially convincing enough to get by. Several hours after Jamir was seen back in Quincy, he was apprehended and taken in for questioning. With his lawyer present to back him up, Jamir, along with the rest of his crew, provided their alibis, got them checked out, and were released within the hour.

The federal investigators pushed the Hooliganz hard, even threatened to do them serious bodily harm, but they stuck to the script, and walked away laughing. So many others took their situation as being the cops were just stupid, or scared to really be crossed with the Hooliganz Crime Gang. But the truth of the matter was the muthafuckers were sharp and on top of their game. They planned a plan that would make them the victor, whenever it came down to it.

The Feds were duped, once again, by the HCG crew, and couldn't do a damn thing about it. However, the Hooliganz were a little worried and cautious about what the Feds would try to pull next. Zamon, Lil One, and Twan were pulled over, four days after their return, and became victims of police brutality. All three of them were cuffed and beaten severely outside the two o'clock BP Gas Station, one night. When Jamir learned of this, he told his crew not to retaliate, at least not immediately, because that would be just what the cops wanted to really do them in. Jamir made them exercise the values of patience and willpower to remain humble. They would get theirs later down the line. Their deaths were already claimed. Right now, what was more important was survival and family, making sure the Feds kept a safe distance.

Meanwhile, Jamir had gotten Harmoni and his son, Lisa and what was left of his valued worldly possessions, and got the hell out of Quincy and their spot in Tallahassee, and moved them to a new place in Georgia. He did not mind driving three hours to get home from doing whatever he had going on throughout the day. All he cared about was keeping his family safe.

After settling his family in at their new place, Jamir decided to spend some much needed quality time with them. He had been longing for the presence of his son, the temper tantrums from Jamaal, and just the smell of his little man. The streets were not in dire need of his presence, at the moment. This was his chill time. This was his family time. Besides, Tilly was busy doing everything she could to see that her shit was organized, and the Hooliganz were taken care of. She was proving her worth as a certified leader and a vicious gangstress.

Jamir still wasn't talking to LaShonda. Their bond had broken, when she withheld the truth from him about who his real father was. She tried reaching out to him, but Jamir wasn't having none of it. He was still hurting. The loss of two fathers was devastating. Then, by some unknown force of action, Jamir found himself being enthralled by the spoken word experience from those such as Tamika Mallory, 2Pac, DMX and even the beloved, Maya Angelou, had become his mental inspirations. When his mother-in-law learned about his new passion for the spoken word, she went and found him one of those bars, where they catered to spoken word lovers. The spot was called Tammy's Bar &

Lounge, and both Lisa and Jamir had visited the place twice already.

After leaving from Hollow's place one day, Jamir decided to swing by Jin-Jin's Chinese restaurant. He was hungry and some shrimp fried rice and egg rolls sounded like a plan. He turned on to Lake Bradford road, listening to some spoken word vibes on audio, through his sound system. When he pulled up on the scene, there was a nice crowd coming in and out of the Chinese joint. He drew some attention, not only because he was pushing a shiny navy blue McLaren F1, but because of what he was listening to. It didn't bother him because he was growing accustomed to the attention. Not everybody had to be listening to NBA Youngboy or No Cap. For the most part, Jamir paid the people no mind, but he did return a few of their stares with a cold one of his own.

People had the misinterpretation that because one was on some humble shit, you either scared of something or a punk, not Jamir. He was fearless and he was a gangster, and a bitch better not take him for a joke.

"Hosanna Wong," said the female, who was leaning against the back of a car, two spaces down from where he had parked.

Jamir paused in mid-step and looked in her direction.

"What you just said?" he asked the female.

She pushed herself away from the car, as she held what looked like a Newport cigarette in her hand. To Jamir, she looked no older than himself, pretty and fashionably dressed, and strangely rough round the edges a little.

"Hosanna Wong," she replied. "That's who you were listening to. She's one helluva poet, isn't she?"

Jamir looked at her in astonishment. "She's a beast," he replied. "I'm surprised you know who that was."

"That's the problem, you don't know me."

"What's your name, beautiful?"

"Nyaisha,"

He nodded. "I'm Jamir."

She grinned sweetly at him. "Nice to meet you, Jamir. I must say, you have excellent taste in the spoken word department. I'm impressed someone of your age is even building with the likes of Hosanna Wong."

"How old do you think I am?"

"Sixteen," she answered.

Jamir said slowly, "Lucky guess. And you?"

What happened next totally knocked Jamir off guard. She suddenly punched him on the shoulder.

"Didn't your momma ever tell you not to ask a woman her age?" she said.

Jamir shrugged with nonchalance.

That day, Jamir met someone, whom he thought was on the same level as him. They stood there talking for quite a while, until her female companion exited the Chinese joint for their car. She and he exchanged numbers, and to his astonishment, she kissed his cheek before finally taking her leave. Nyaisha had made him blush.

That day, where Jamir thought he met someone special, he had no clue of the trouble she actually was. Nyaisha was more than what met the eye. She was a conning bitch, and Jamir would soon find out.

Chapter 22

It was just Monica and Danielle in the room when the door opened and LaShonda entered the room. The conversation stopped instantly, when they saw who it was. Then Monica shot up to her feet, at once.

"Sit your ass down, Monica. Ain't. Nobody. Fixin'. To. Do. Nothin'," said LaShonda as she waved the other woman off. "Hev is my baby, just as much as she is yours. So, chill the hell out, woman."

Monica wasn't trying to hear none of that shit LaShonda was talking about. She hurried over to put herself between the bed and the possible threat.

"Monica..."

"No. You listen to me, LaShonda." Monica glared at her with a dark piercing gaze. "Before I let somethin' else happen to my daughter, I'll die before I let that go down."

"I came to see my baby," said LaShonda. "The rest of that mess you talking about is irrelevant, Monica."

"Don't test me, LaShonda."

Monica didn't budge, nor did she blink.

"I love you, Monica. You are my sista, bitch. I know thangs ain't been on the up between us because of this mess between Hev and her brothaz, but I'm here to make amends wit' you, Monica, not fight and complicate thangs more." Then LaShonda lost her cool and burst into tears.

"I done loss my baby, too," she cried miserably. "Jay is gone."

At hearing those words, Danielle stood up to her feet and made her way over towards the two women. She then wrapped her arms around LaShonda, which made her cry even harder.

"What happened to Jamir?" Monica asked.

No answer.

"LaShonda?"

Monica reached to take ahold of LaShonda in a one arm embrace, and pressed her forehead against her sista's shoulder, as it shook in anguish.

Minutes later, LaShonda's cries subsided, and she was helped into one of the chairs next to the bed. It was then that Danielle inquired about Jamir's situation, and LaShonda told them about their falling out with one another and that she was dead to him now.

"He won't even answer my calls," said LaShonda. "I haven't spoken to him in over a month."

"Wit somethin' like that, LaShonda, you gotta let time heal on its own. Look at what you kept from him all these years. Jay has a right to be angry wit' you."

"He acts like he doesn't love me anymore," said LaShonda.

"He loves you," said Danielle.

She hadn't heard from Shamar since his escape, weeks ago. She too should be angry with him as well, but she had to keep a level head. She knew all about Aliyah not being LJ's child, but Shamar's, which was one of the reasons she was there today. She had always looked at the little girl in quiet wonder at the strange resemblance she had with Shamar. Danielle just never believed that he and Heaven would be intimately involved with one another, until just recently, when she visited with Anya and saw her man in the child's face.

Aliyah was no doubt Shamar's daughter, and it hurt Danielle to her heart that he kept that truth from her.

Everybody seemed to have a secret or two. These secrets hurt.

"Where is Jay now?" asked Monica curiously.

LaShonda shrugged. "I don't know."

"You tried calling Harmoni or her mama?"

"They changed their numbers."

Then LaShonda went on to tell them how none of the Hooliganz she had run across would provide her any useful information.

"It's like he turned them against me, too," she said.

"No," said Danielle. "They're just acting on the orders that were given to them."

"Yeah, right." LaShonda wasn't convinced.

After LaShonda had tired herself of talking about her situation, Monica forgave her sister and gave her the updates on her own situation. Everything was going well up until someone else came knocking. When Chad came into the room, followed by Heaven's assigned nurse, Shequita Johnson, he frowned upon seeing LaShonda, and she frowned back. It wasn't lost on her that Marlon's baby brother blamed her son for his reasons for being there.

"What she doing here?" Chad asked sourly.

"Minding my own goddamn business, nigga. You don't want to test this shit right now, Chad, or I swear on everything I love you gon' be buried right next…"

When he was about to respond, Monica bolted to her feet to prevent him from doing so.

"Stop. LaShonda, that's enough of that mess." snapped Monica.

"I'm just saying," LaShonda folded her arms stubbornly.

Chad might have assumed she was speaking out of anger alone, but little did he know, LaShonda was dead ass serious. She would kill his ass right where he stood.

Chad saw that killer in her dark brown eyes, and warned himself not to test her farther. Then Monica hugged him and thanked Chad for stopping by to show some moral support.

"She's my niece," he replied.

Chad wasn't the street, gangsta type, like his big brother was, but he wasn't afraid to push his weight around. He didn't just have the pretty boy looks, but had a little spunk, too.

"You also have a nephew, too, Chad," said LaShonda.

He turned a hard gaze on her. "What?"

"You heard what she said, Chad. You have Marlon's son, too."

The look on Marlon's face was priceless. "His son? Who?"

"My son," said LaShonda.

"Jamir," Danielle chimed in. "Jay and Hev are biological siblings, Chad. So yeah, you got a nephew, too."

Chad looked from one mother to the other, and they both gave him the same expression in return.

"I thought… I mean, how the hell that shit happened?"

"Sexual intercourse between man and woman, Chad," said LaShonda in a mocking tone of voice.

Then she decided to tell him about the time when Marlon caught her at her most vulnerable and she fell for his charms. By this time, Heaven was almost two years old and Monica had already kicked him to the curb. LaShonda admitted her faults, and Monica accepted her apology and offered her forgiveness, both of them understanding how dangerously persuasive Marlon was. A wicked smirked appeared on Chad's face at the thought of his big brother bagging two bad, beautiful women, who were also friends.

"What's so funny, Chad?" asked Danielle.

"You don't wanna know," he said.

He visited with them for another twenty minutes, before he hugged and kissed Monica on the cheek. Then, as he was headed for the door, he stopped and looked back at LaShonda for a second. He then turned back around to her and pulled her into his embrace.

"Thank you for keepin' it real, LaShonda. Just give my nephew some time and he'll come around, because one thing I know about being a son," he replied. "He will always love his mama, no matter what."

"Shamar is a prime example," said Danielle.

Chad nodded. He knew all too well what Shamar had to go through, being the son of a well-known drug addict. MoMo had been his joy and his pain, all at the same time. When he finally left, LaShonda sighed deeply and reclaimed her seat at Heaven's bedside.

"I wonder if he knew," said Monica.

"Knew what?"

"That Marlon didn't die that night, five years ago," Monica replied.

All LaShonda could do was shake her head. Then she paused and looked over at Monica in puzzlement. "Come again?"

"So you don't know, huh?"

"Know what?"

Monica frowned at her. "The reason why my daughter is layin' up in this bed right now, that's what to fuckin' know." Then she told her everything.

LaShonda already knew what the story was, she just wanted to hear Monica tell it in her own words.

Chapter 23

It was a cool breeze coming off the Hudson River, as LJ sat on the back of the bench, rolling up a Backwood, staring out into the darkness of the water. When he turned around, he saw a white car pull up. A female got out and walked over to him. She had on a pantsuit and pumps, and sat down on the bench next to LJ's feet.

"What's up?" LJ replied.

"Don't mind me, sweetheart. I come here often to unleash, and do some soul-searching," she said.

"Sounds like you keep a complicated life." LJ fired up the blunt and inhaled deeply.

"Complicated is an understatement, sweetheart."

"Tell me about it then."

She finally gazed up at him, and stared at LJ for a long moment. "Your accent. You're a southerner. You have this down south twang thing going on. Where are you from?" she asked politely.

LJ hit the blunt slowly, before responding. "I'm from a place where even the sun is cold."

"Georgia?"

"Nope."

"Tennessee?"

He shook his head no. "Stop guessing. I asked you a question first. What's so complicated?" said LJ.

Before she decided to respond, the white woman plucked the blunt from between his fingers and put it to her full lips, for a puff. One hit was all it took to send her into a coughing fit. LJ smirked and began slapping her against her slender back. She attempted another pull from the blunt, and the second went nicely, and she handed it back to him.

"I hadn't smoked that shit since college," she said in this comical tone of voice that made her sound a little slurred in speech.

"So you're a school girl?"

"Yep."

"What was you studying?"

"Criminal law," she told him. "Twelve years of representing criminals and subjecting myself into fallin' for one of them assholes, and risking my whole career for nothing."

"For nothin'?"

She swayed in her seat as she gazed out over the water before her. "For nothing," she whispered.

"What happened?"

"I allowed my emotional attachment to overpower my rational thinking, that's what happened. I fell for a gangster, and once I gave him my all for these past two years, and granted him his freedom back, he left me out to the wolves, and I'll be damned if I let him use me like that and get away with it. I want his black ass to burn in hell for that," she said out of anger, and LJ would have sworn he felt her wrath intensify the atmosphere around them.

So this dude was black, thought LJ. Of all the people to interrupt his solitude tonight, it had to be a brokenhearted lawyer. But instead of dismissing her and going on about his business, LJ slid down to sit next to her, and took her into his arms. Then she cried upon his shoulder. LJ kissed her... and that's all it took to have her moaning and screaming in intense pleasure, thirty minutes later, as he pounded her pussy from the back, along the backseat of her car. LJ was giving her that thug love, and he didn't know this bitch from a can of paint. But they both found the desired resolution to their problem in the wake of one another's passion, in the heat of the night. The cure of a good nut to take the edge off.

"Amelia," she whispered.

"Huh?'

"My name," she replied, while snuggled up against him, in the backseat of her car. "It's Amelia Graham."

"And my name is Leonardo Jones."

"Really? Your name is Leonardo?" she asked.

He kissed her on the tip of her pointy nose, as an answer to her question.

Amelia had excelled in school and had ultimately graduated from the University of Texas Law School, in the top ten percent of her class. Law was the profession her father had chosen for her. Then, eventually, it became an exercise that delighted and intrigued Amelia. Her curious mind took pleasure in delving into its intricacies. She was well prepared to do what she must to survive the pressures that life had thrown her way, and LJ would be that tool that would help her mend her broken spirit.

"Wanna know where my complicated life derived from?" LJ replied, after a momentary thought process.

"What makes your life complicated?"

"Trust. The girl I loved fooled me into believing that her daughter was my child, but the whole time it was her best friend's daughter instead."

"Her best friend?"

He nodded.

"Damn," she muttered. "That's fucked up."

What was more fucked up about it was the fact that he had known the truth, way before Shamar had confronted him about it earlier, and he still managed to get the best of Shamar, who was currently unconsciousness in the trunk of his car.

"Yeah," LJ said thoughtfully. "That was really fucked up."

What did Shamar expect from confrontation? To be forgiven for betraying his trust?

"So what now?" Amelia asked him.

"I don't know," he said.

"Tell me about them, Leonardo. I want to know everything you are willing to give me in the form of trust. Let me see what you saw in the matter."

"You're tryna be a lawyer right now."

"No," she said. "I'm trying to begin a friendship."

He couldn't argue with that, at all. LJ told her what he had been battling in his heart for so long. He had been patiently waiting to see who would bring the truth to him first. It so happened to be Shamar and now look where his actions had gotten him.

"Leonardo?" Amelia replied, when he was done telling her everything about how he felt about the situation.

He did not answer her.

"Sounds like to me, her and him didn't want to intentionally cause you grief. She had trusted her best friend to give her what she probably felt she wouldn't be able to give you, when that time came."

"And what's that?"

"A sexual experience, where all her mistakes would not be judged by him, but encouraged to the point that, when it was her and your time, it would be more fulfilling, because then she would know just what to do to please her man, which was you," said Amelia. "I know it all sounds crazy, but I very much doubt either one of them wanted to hurt you intentionally, Leonardo. So, sweetheart, I think you should forgive your brother and appreciate him for the experience. And together you both can work your difference through loving and appreciating that beautiful child, as a team."

LJ actually took he words into consideration.

"Forgive your brother for his actions, and if you still have any love left for her, let that love show. Be a more positive, yet humble, example to loved ones, sweetheart. I know you can. I feel your energy," said Amelia.

"Can I show you something, Amelia?"

"What?"

"C'mon," LJ slithered out of the car and extended his hand towards her. "It's just over here," he said.

After helping her out of the back seat of her car, Amelia situated her clothes for a brief second, and then followed LJ over to another car, parked several yards away. There, she watched as LJ moved towards the trunk of the car and opened it for her to see inside. When she did, her heart lurched with instant fear.

"Oh my God! Leonardo! Is he dead?" she panicked, and looked like she was ready to flee, but she held her ground and stood firm against him.

"That's Shamar right there," he gestured.

"Your brother?" she gasped.

He nodded. "And it's all because of you, he will now live to see another day," said LJ.

Then he shook Shamar awake and reached out his hand to him. Shamar stared up at him with cautious eyes, and Amelia feared he was about to spring forward in attack mode.

"It's ok, Shamar. He forgives you," Amelia said in a shaky voice, as she watched Shamar wrestle with the thought of whether he should trust LJ or not.

"You better thank her for saving your ass, nigga. Get the fuck outta the damn trunk before I lock your big headed ass back in it," said LJ. "C'mon, brah."

Reluctantly, Shamar slapped his palm against LJ's in a grip hold, and then he was pulled from the confines of the trunk. When looking at the two brothers standing before one another, it made Amelia tearful to know where their love had come from, where it would go from there.

"So, what's it's gonna be, Leonardo?" said Amelia, nudging him in the side with her elbow.

"Who are you?" Shamar looked at her and said.

"Your guardian angel," she quipped.

LJ took a deep breath. "We all we got, brah. Real shit. You fucked my girl, but I know you didn't do it with cruel intentions. She just trusted you more."

"I didn't, my nigga. That's on Vee," said Shamar.

"We still boys?" asked LJ, hopeful

"Naw, muthafucker, we ain't boys," Shamar blurted out, and Amelia flinched at his sudden outburst.

Then he broke out into a devilish grin. "We Hooliganz," he said.

"For life," LJ said.

The two brothaz hugged each other.

Amelia looked confused. "Hooliganz?" she replied. "What's that?"

Chapter 24

When June, the bartender, called Tilly and told her to come to the bar and what for, she dropped everything she was doing to get there. Tilly had just left from seeing her ex-boyfriend's brother, Tec, about some business she had in mind. Upon her arrival, with two of her Royals flanking her, Tilly found June behind the bar nursing a beer for himself.

"Where is she?" asked Tilly.

The bartender nodded towards the back of the room, which led to a back room, only for Royal Mafia.

"Who's she back there wit', June?" she asked.

"She's alone, just like I told you."

"Good lookin' out, big man."

June said, "The only reason why I called is because I know your old man, and he was a real cool player. Plus, I know you got Hev's best interest at heart wit' whateva you got going on out there. Ya feel me, lil Beanie?"

He referred to her by her father's name, Beanie, who was lying dead in his grave, over at Sunnyville Cemetery. Tilly extended her fist and June bumped it with his own, respectively.

For an early Thursday evening, the bar was jumping with its usuals. Some old school Al Green was booming from the sound system. Two players talked cash shit over at the pool tables area. The place was lively, and here was Tilly, anticipating murder in the same space.

When Tilly and her Royals entered through the door into the backroom, they saw Rhonda occupying the space. Without even warning her, Tilly pulled out her butterfly knife and armed its blade. This was Rhonda Da Steppa, who had been one of Skarr's best recruits, and who turned out to be the last one left. Rhonda had been in the process of pouring herself another glass of Grey Goose from the private bar adjoining the rear end of the room. She was sitting down at the poker table, already looking like she'd drank more than her fair share. She was literally swaying in her seat drunkenly, as she slowly refilled her glass for one more round.

Tilly slid into the chair across from Rhonda, and upon seeing who it was, Rhonda grinned over at her, as if she found the situation funny or something. Both Sheena and NaiNai took up positions behind Rhonda's chair, and waited with their guns at ready.

"You came to kill me, too, Tilly?" said Rhonda. Although she was a plus size female, Rhonda maintained her weight and carried it well, without the sloppiness, like some others.

"You chose to ride wit' the other side," Tilly said.

"That's where you wrong at, Tilly. I was only loyal to the money. When Skarr recruited me, I ain't even have a pot to piss in. She gave me hope, Tilly. Now she's dead and I'm back at square one."

"Square one?"

"Yep."

"So you're telling me all that shit Skarr and Baiyina had you out here doing wasn't compensated for? Are you broke, Rhonda?"

"Not entirely," said Rhonda slurring. "Only got enough to last me a lil while. Why?"

"So money is your motivation?"

"Always was, and always will be, Tilly."

"Not the purpose for which Royal Mafia stands for?" Tilly figured she already knew the answer to that. "Do you even know what Royal Mafia stands for?"

"No," Rhonda admitted.

With the roll of her eyes, Tilly lifted her gaze up at NaiNai, standing behind her.

"What do we stand for, Nai?"

"Empowerment. Growth. And fearlessness."

"And what are we Sheena?"

"A sisterhood built on principles and morals and oppression against those who dare to oppress against us," said Sheena.

"And what is our ultimate law?"

"Dishonor," said NaiNai. "Punishable by death."

Tilly nodded approvingly.

"You know what, Rhonda? I can't even be mad at you. I can't blame you for being led wrong. I believe you, Rhonda. That's why I'm not gonna kill you. All you wanted to do was make your paper," she said. "But this is what I will do for you Rhonda."

"What's that, Tilly?"

"I'm going to give you one opportunity to choose, your loyalty to Royal Mafia or your loyalty to the money?" Tilly stared at her in an unsteady posture.

Sheena lifted her banger and aimed it at the back of Rhonda's head. Just as soon as she said the wrong word, it would be the last word she ever spoke. When Rhonda opened her mouth to speak, the door across the room opened and all eyes shifted in its direction at the person who suddenly walked through it.

"Well I be damned," muttered Tilly at the unexpected presence of the last person she expected to see.

It was Toby. One look at her cousin and Tilly could see that Toby wasn't looking too happy.

"Toby," Rhonda bellowed, managing to stand up on two wobbly legs, appearing, for a second, as if she was about to tip over.

"I know damn well y'all wasn't about to dome check this drunk bitch back here," said Toby.

She approached them and stopped to look at Rhonda in contempt.

"What's the issue wit' this one, cuz?"

"She was ridin' wit' Skarr and em," said Tilly.

"Oh yeah?"

"But," Tilly gave her cousin the lowdown on the situation and finished with, "She was about to choose just before you came in, cuz."

"So, what's it gon' be, Rhonda?" Toby asked.

Just like she knew she would, Rhonda chose Royal Mafia. That's when she ordered NaiNai and Sheena to remove Rhonda from the room and sober her up. After they left, Tilly gestured for her cousin to take the seat Rhonda had been occupying, moments ago. Toby took her seat, and together, they say across from each other as a thick silence passed between them.

"I can see somethin' is botherin' you, Toby. What is it, cuz?"

"I'm about to turn myself in, Tilly?"

"Turn yourself in?" Tilly was astonished by what she had just heard Toby say, but she was too familiar with what was going on with Kiara being locked up because of the rap she took to protect Toby. "You're serious," she said in a low voice, filled with warm emotion.

"I don't got no other choice, Tilly."

"What about Ty?"

"He knows. And, of course, he doesn't like it. But I'd rather it be me locked up in there than her. Shit happens, cuz, and it done happened to me. I gotta do what's right about this shit," said Toby straightforwardly.

Tilly's eyes welled up with tears.

"You better not cry for me," said Toby.

"I can't help it, cuz. I love you, bitch! What the hell we gon' do wit'out you?"

"The same shit you been doing when I wasn't here. I shouldn't have to tell you how you should handle your business, Tilly, only that you should be careful and analyze everything before you make a concrete decision on it. You know what's best for the team, but most of all, what's best for yourself, too."

Tilly was quiet longer than expected.

"Don't let them come back in here and see you like that, Tilly," warned Toby in a firm tone.

Her gaze was sharp and her heart full of realness. Right then, White Boy Ty entered the room and leaned back against the wall closest to the door. He shoved his hands into his pockets and stared longingly over at them. That mothafucker looked devastated. Toby's turning herself in to the authorities so willingly was a hard pill for all of them to swallow.

"We have a plan," said Toby.

"What plan, Toby? If you think that shit Dee had us pull gon' work again, then you got anotha thang coming. Them crackaz are not about to take no more losses. You go in there, and they gon' hide your ass so deep under that muthafucker that God can't find you."

Toby kept her cool. She glared over in Ty's direction and willed her heart to be still.

"I gotta do what I gotta do, cuz," said Toby.

Then she opened out her hand to her across the table. Tilly took it slowly and her cousin squeezed it reassuringly. "C'mon, walk me out to the car."

"Fuck that. I'm walking you all the way through the door of that police station," said Tilly.

Shit was about to really get real. Toby was making the ultimate sacrifice, her freedom for Kiara's freedom. She was about to own up to her crime to save a life that was very special to her. It was a cold reality. It was frightening.

Chapter 25

Toby's next destination wasn't the jailhouse, but directly to the Quincy hospital to visit with Heaven, one last time. When White Boy Ty thought it was a bad idea, Toby assured him that her heart was at peace. Heaven was her sister, and she was not going another day forward, without making amends with her. Plus, Royal Mafia was now under her command, for the time being. She would be well-protected, if anything other than what's under her control presented itself.

At the hospital, Blanca and Crystal were guarding the room outside Heaven's door. When they saw Toby step around the corner, both of their eyes widened with surprise.

"What's up, Bee?" said Toby, dapping up the Royal before her.

"I see you, girl. So you back wit' us again?"

"For now," Toby told her.

"What does that mean?" asked Crystal.

Toby reached up and stroked Crystal's face lovingly. "Tilly'll fill you both in on what's going on."

Then she touched Blanca's shoulder before stepping through to walk inside the room. Upon her entrance, LaShonda looked up at her and a deep expression settled on her face. She was in the company of Anya, Aliyah, Malik, and another female that Toby knew nothing about. She was a white girl with designer braids, thick in the hips and cute, but also serious looking in a way. Upon closer inspection, Toby saw that the unknown female was of a mulatto flavor.

"Toby," LaShonda stood up and opened out her arms to her. "Welcome back," she said, and squeezed Toby in a long embrace.

"Not for long, I won't be," said Toby as she recognized that Monica was not present. Right then, Aliyah Renee separated herself from Anya and tottered over to Toby, with her arms spread out for some affection, too. Toby scooped her up and gave her sweet mini kisses.

"Where's Monica?" she turned her attention back to LaShonda.

"I sent her home for a little while to rest and clean herself up for a change," said LaShonda.

"She's fallin' apart, huh?"

Anya nodded. "She doesn't even seem like herself anymore," she replied. "This mess is taking a major toll on her. It is wit' everybody who cares about what's going on." She shot Toby an accusing look that made her uneasy.

"It has really changed us all," said the mulatto female, who was in the process of entertaining four year old Malik with YouTube videos on her smartphone.

The look Toby gave her next prompted the stranger to explain who she was. Her name was Angelica Richardson, and she was a student at FAMU College, majoring in journalism. She and Heaven had met during Heaven's senior year in high school, but always kept in touch. Angelica, annoyed by the whole situation, wished she had the power to wake Heaven up and make things back the way they were.

After hearing her out, Toby sat baby girl back down on the floor and moved over to Heaven's bedside. She stared down on her for a very long time. Then she leaned in to place a gentle kiss upon her cheek and forehead.

"I love you, Hev. Fuck the rest of this bullshit that's going on," said Toby. "We family. You'll always be my little sista. Now you gotta fight this shit and wake up. We need you back in the game, boo. Tighten up. Stop playin' em games and wake the fuck up and let us see that beautiful smile again. Royal Mafia." She allowed a tear to escape her eyes and swiped it away.

Anya was quietly crying, too. Aliyah saw this and reached her chubby little hand up to wipe her tears away. "No cry," she whispered animatedly. "No sad. Stop."

Blanca then entered the room and stared at Toby in disbelief. "You're really turning yourself in?"

"Huh? Doing what now? What is she talkin' about turning in?" LaShonda replied, looking from Blanca to Toby, who was now staring back at her gravely.

Tilly entered the room looking heartbroken.

"She's about to go turn herself in to the police to free Mz. Kiara," said Blanca.

"What?"

"I'm not surprised," said LaShonda.

Then Toby explained to them her situation and how she felt about Kiara going to prison for something she did. But LaShonda already knew it wasn't Kiara who murdered Meesha and Pumpkin, nor was she the killer of Heather Peacock. Her respect level for Toby went up another degree because of the decision she was making to own up to her crime.

"It is what it is," said Toby. "But it's not over for me by a long shot," she smirked.

"Lemme guess," said Anya. "You got a plan."

"There's always a plan," said LaShonda. Then she pulled Toby back into her arms again. "You a souljah, Toby. I respect what you are doing."

"Does Delani know?" asked Anya.

Toby nodded. "He was understanding about it. Delani had been more patient wit' me," she said.

When it was time to go, Toby took her leave with dignity. She held her head high and walked out of the hospital, without a backwards glance. White Boy Ty met her outside the main entrance and escorted her back to the car. Fifteen minutes later, Detective Angie Galloway met Toby and her cousin, Tilly, at the front door of the police station. Ty watched from the car across the street. He wanted so badly to go snatch her ass back up and get her away from there, but he kept his composure. White Boy Ty was frantic.

"Are you sure this what you want to do, Toby?" Angie asked her the moment she met them at the door.

"It's your cousin I'm saving," she said.

The older woman nodded. "True," said Angie.

She then took Toby by the arm, looked at Tilly, and told her that it was best if she remained outside. Then Angie opened the door and led her inside. When that door closed, White Boy Ty dropped his head and closed his eyes. Tilly stood stuck on stupid. It was going down. The ultimate sacrifice.

Chapter 26

Meanwhile, Roxy was riding in a black Acura NSX, with a Mac 90 assault rifle sitting on the passenger seat. She was following behind another car, which was a burgundy colored Dodge Challenger, with two people riding inside, and Roxy was waiting for the perfect opportunity to press play.

Roxy was a known killer and drug dealer from the Bronx. She was twenty-seven years old, with a criminal record so long you could make a floor rug out of it. She'd recently come home from doing a bid out west, for violent crimes. The bitch was dangerous, a lost soul. She lived for and *loved* that violent shit and drama like some bitches love going shopping, but she was nothing like her big brother Dank, who was currently in the Feds for gang violence and fraud charges. Her big brother was a cold-hearted nigga, without a conscience, and the only thing on his mind was banging his Blood Gang sect.

The person she was following was Keith "Hoodie" Thompson, another one who had recently got out of jail. Hood was responsible for killin' his own brother, Qay, who had been one of the closet friends Roxy had. After he went to trial and won, he was released back to the street. Roxy knew he would end up being her next victim. Regardless what he and Qay was going through, that was still Roxy's nigga, and for that, she would avenge his death rightfully. Qay would have done it for her. That nigga was solid. He was genuine.

Hood was no dummy. He was a killer, just like her. He once had been one of the few street niggas that she actually admired, growing up. They were from the same hood, and Roxy didn't give a fuck about that. The nigga had to die. She followed the car in front of her from the game room on 8th and 132nd Streets all the way now onto 151st Street and Convent, uptown. In the background, as she drove, Roxy was vibing to the gangsta tunes of rapper EST Gee, and itching to pull the trigger.

The Dodge Challenger rolled through the neighborhood, with Hood riding shotgun, obviously smoking weed, and possibly drinking. He was a fool for Crown Royal, and Roxy was hoping he was enjoying that last drink. Just when she was beginning to grow inpatient with the wait, the car up ahead turned onto 119th and Lenox Ave. She reluctantly made the turn next. When she did, Roxy was suddenly alarmed, when she saw the car come to a halt in the middle of the street. Roxy's eyes widened when she saw Hood jump out of the car with a Draco.

Relentlessly, he began drilling holes in the car as he proceeded to walk down on her. She threw herself across the seat for her own weapon. The look on Hood's face as he filled the car with bullet holes was of pure rage. She could actually see the murder in his eyes.

When Roxy sprang back up, she had her Mac-90 in possession. Then without so much as a second thought, she upped the assault rifle and begin busting back through the windshield. She didn't care about the close proximity, all she cared about was shooting back. That cost her two slugs to her body. The first slug hit her in the chest of her bulletproof vest. The second one tore a chunk out of her right shoulder. Her rage and adrenaline kept her finger on the trigger. It didn't take Hood long to see that he needed to get missing, and he did. He ran back for his car, hopped in it, and sped away. Hood was gone.

By this time, Roxy was so agonized with pain that it made her dizzy. She fought for breath, and it felt like a struggle to breathe. Roxy made an attempt to drive away, but then realized that wouldn't be happening. Hood had shot out the front tires, and somehow damaged the car's engine during the shooting. She then decided to get out of the car and try to make a run for it, but that was the last thing she would remember before everything went dark. She had lost and Hood had gotten away. Just another typical day in Harlem, New York.

Chapter 27

"What are we doing, Bizzy?" Youngin asked, the second his brother exited from the bathroom. Bizzy didn't answer him right away. He made his way back to the front of their brownstone apartment. There lay Roxy on the living room floor, still unconscious. When Youngin looked at her, a worried expression spread across his face.

"First of all, Bizzy," said Youngin. "We was in total violation for even stepping outside during the daytime anyway. Then we don' got this bitch outta a jam on some shit we don't even got nothin' to do wit'."

"I know her, brah," Bizzy replied.

Youngin shot him a stern look. "You know this bitch?"

He nodded.

It had happened a little over a week ago. Bizzy, Shamar, and Skinny were out in the city one night, just chillin' and trying to get the lay of the land. It was on a Wednesday night, and they were passing through the Bronx Community College way. They turned into the entrance of a nearby gas station, and both Shamar and Skinny went inside the station. Bizzy had remained behind, where Roxy had eventually rolled up on the scene across from him. She parked her Lexus Jeep on the other side of the gas pump. When she hopped down from the jeep, something had fallen out onto the ground in the process. Bizzy didn't notice it until he had shifted on his feet, and she was halfway to the gas station building's entrance. Bizzy stepped between the two pumps to pick it up and discovered that it was a ski mask.

Minutes later, when Roxy exited the station with a bottle of Mountain Dew in her hand, Bizzy took the opportunity to approach her with his findings.

"You dropped this," said Bizzy, presenting what he found,

Roxy stopped and looked at the black ski mask in his hand. "It must have fell when I got out," she said.

"It did."

"Thank you," she accepted it back humbly.

"But my question is," Bizzy handed her the ski mask and she had made her way back over to her truck. Again, he stepped between the pump and said, "Isn't it a little too hot for ski masks right now?"

"It's a cold world out there," she said.

"But why, though? I mean, who would want to hide something so beautiful behind a ski mask anyway?"

Roxy stared at him for a long moment, her pretty green eyes sharp and searching. She didn't respond to his question, just saluted him, got back into her truck, and left.

Now, as he stared down at Roxy laying on his living room floor, Bizzy shook his head in discontentment.

"So, what now?" asked Youngin.

"We wait."

"Wait the fuck for what?"

Bizzy said, "Until she wake up."

The bullet wound to her shoulder was a through and through injury that Bizzy had stripped her shirt off to clean her wound. He wasn't no doctor or anything, but he knew enough to make sure she was taken care of, which is why Bizzy kept a selection of medical supplies on hand, in case of emergencies, where going to the hospital was a no-go. If anything was too serious, he could go kidnap the doctor himself and bring him in, but that was only if things were that critical. Youngin was not feeling this shit, but he trusted

Bizzy to make the wisest decisions. He was the thinker of the two, the humbled but more dangerous one.

"So, we wait," muttered Youngin very slowly.

"That's right."

"And what if that other muthafucker finds out we got her in here and decides to come finish her off?"

"He won't."

"What makes you so sure about that, Bizzy?"

Before Bizzy could answer that, the code knock at the front door alerted them that their own had arrived. When Youngin answered the door, he found both Rikah and Booby standing out on the doorstep.

"The hell is going on up in here?" said Rikah, when she walked into the apartment and saw Roxy lying on the floor.

"Ask him," Youngin gestured towards Bizzy.

"Biz?" Rikah put her hands on her hips.

He told her what was going on, and Rikah gave him a look that made him feel very uncomfortable. Meanwhile, Youngin was telling Booby in sign language what the situation was. Booby seemed excited by this, and nudged Roxy's leg with his foot.

"So now you're Captain-Save-A-Hoe, Biz? What you did was reckless, and you know it. And you know I have to report this to Dee, right?" Rikah said.

"So what?" he retorted.

She glared at him. "Really Bizzy?"

Bizzy said, "I did what I felt was right, Rikah. I know I don't know this bitch, but there's something about her, though. I do believe in consciences. A bitch like this can be useful towards our mission, wit what we tryna do."

"She's a marked bitch, stupid."

"Yeah, that's true," Bizzy shrugged. "She's a marked bitch, but I still think she could be a great asset to the crew. Fuck that. What's done can't be undone. Y'all don't have to deal with her. I will on my own. I got this."

"We got this," Youngin corrected him.

With the shake of her head, Rikah looked down at Roxy and saw that she was a very attractive woman. Small in stature, but something told her she was huge in personality.

"This your mess, Biz," said Rikah. "The both of you hard-headed ass niggaz," she jabbed an accusing finger in the direction of Bizzy and Youngin. "Y'all better clean this shit up because, if it jeopardizes our mission, just know that both of you will be punished by bloodshed."

"Say no more," said Bizzy.

"I'm not."

Roxy, who had been halfway conscious of what was going on around her, heard everything that was said. Her life had been spared by a total stranger, and to her surprise, the stranger was none other than the very same nigga she dreamed about.

Chapter 28

It had been two days since Toby turned herself in, and still Kiara's release was not granted. For whatever reason, she was not let go. There had to be a valid explanation, and sure enough, Vivian Evanovich was about to find out. When she got the call about Toby turning herself in, she reacted immediately. She had been out of town in Thomasville, Georgia, representing the nephew of a close friend of hers on a home invasion murder case. Vivian was a beast, her loyalty to the people who hired her services ranged throughout three different states. The woman was the female Ben Crump. She was something fierce indeed.

Harold was beside himself with worry. Ever since Kiara went in, he'd been dying inside. For better or worse, those were the vows he made, and Lord knows Harold was dealing with the worst. He had lost a son through death, the other through his life as a fugitive on the run, and now his beloved wife to the very same system that took their sons.

Harold believed they were playing games and holding Kiara out of spite because of Delani and what happened. It was known that Quincy Police Department and their judicial system were crooked and very adamant about disregarding policies and laws to get what they wanted. They played hardball. Them muthafuckers were criminals, too, in their own way. The judicial system was full of demons.

When Vivian returned his call, she not only had bad news, but very disturbing information for him. Apparently, a relative or close friend of one of the victims Kiara was suspected of killing lived in the same female unit as she. There was a real live sneak attack on Kiara, and she suffered severely. She had suffered a broken jaw, cracked ribs, and a few slashes to the face by her assailant's homemade razor knife. On top of that, Kiara was also charged with assault on a law enforcement officer and staff nurse, plus possession of three ounces of heroin and cocaine. That very moment, she was detained and now waiting to go back before the judge again.

"All that is some straight up bullshit," said Harold furiously.

"I second that opinion," Vivian said to him.

"So, what are you going to do about it?"

"I have a few things in mind, Mr. Bradwell."

"Well, you need to see that those thangs gets done because my wife don't belong in there. You see what's going on," he stressed to her. "And please make sure they don't put her back in that unit wit' all those other women."

"I can arrange that for you."

"Please do," he pleaded.

Harold spoke with the lawyer for another few minutes and ended their connection. He shut his eyes and leaned his head back against the headrest of his Dodge Ram truck. He fought back against the tears that threatened to burst from his face. The situation with Kiara scared him. There was no doubt in his mind that she was scared, too.

"Just be strong, honey. It's gon' be okay," whispered Harold in his own grief.

He was now contemplating gathering up his own army to go break his dear wife out of jail. A couple of tears squeezed through the cracks of his agony and Harold just let them roll down his face. His silent cries were interrupted by a sudden tapping sound against the driver side window. He opened his eyes and looked to find Angie standing there. She stared at him for a moment to discern what was happening, then she hurried around to the other side to hop in. The whole while Harold had been parked outside the Gadsden County jail, where his wife was being held. He already had gone inside to raise hell, but was sent away worse than he arrived.

Angie got in the passenger side of the truck and immediately took his hand into her own. She could feel the rage traveling through his body, just by touching him.

"They hurt her in there," he said.

"I know," she said quietly.

A momentary silence passed between them.

"But I'ma get Princess and Naomi back for what they did to her, Harold. Rest assured I will handle it, even if I have to reach out to them from the inside.

"You can do that?" he asked.

"I'm the law, Harold. This is my jurisdiction. I can get it done. I will get it done."

He was about to challenge her authority on the matter of her allowing the Feds to come and take his sons away, but Harold knew enough to see that that matter was beyond her pay grade, because once the Feds were involved, then there wasn't much that she could do to prevent it from happening.

"I got a few favors owed to me that could get paid off in those two bitches blood," Angie added.

"Who are they?"

"They're Royals from Heaven's crew," she said.

Harold frowned at the revelation.

"But not any of Hev's actual recruits because they came afterwards. My main man, Jerome McNeil, works as a captain on the second shift," she said thoughtfully.

"Jerome from over by the pecan house? Big Twan old boy?"

She nodded. "If it had been his shift, that shit woulda never went down the way it did. But this is what you need to be aware of, Harold. A lot of the officials are under extreme pressure right now wit' Internal Affairs and they're being pushed to go the extra mile to set an example."

"By planting drugs on Kay in an attempt to prevent her from getting off on a murder case that Toby owned up to? C'mon, Angie. You know damn well that's bullshit."

"It's Delani they really want, Harold. Him and his crew."

"Okay," Harold waited.

"They will somehow try to use her to get to him, and try and double-cross them both in the process.

"Can you stop it?"

"I can damn sure try."

"Don't try, Angie," said Harold as he turned his weary eyes on her. "I'ma need you to do it," he demanded. "If you still love her, like I hope you do, then you need to go in there and represent Kiara."

"I am," she promised. "And Harold?"

"What?"

"I still love you, too," Angie replied.

This time, when Harold looked at her, he saw something else in her eyes that made him shiver under her gaze.

"Do you still love me?"

Harold opened his mouth, but nothing came out. Did he still love her? Of course, he would always love Angie Galloway. She was his first. They had shared something special. She leaned in and kissed him. He didn't pull back, but he damn sure should have because allowing her that little power would make things much more complicated. It already had. The power of attraction was a dangerous game. It was deadly.

Chapter 29

The 40/40 Club was one of the hottest strip clubs in New York, and Hazel was having a ball, drinking with her two best friends, Mona and Yvonnie. She barely spent time in New York with her friends, since she moved away to attend college at Clark Atlanta in Georgia, but tonight, she was glad she came out.

From across the room, Hazel noticed this fine, young, black god, just lounging and nursing a red solo cup. She thought he seemed strangely familiar, but couldn't quite remember where she knew him from. He was dressed in the latest Amir labels, and his swag was on point. What also intrigued her was the fact that he wasn't making it rain, like the rest of the fellas. He wasn't entertaining the dancers. He wasn't trying to be seen. He was just on chill.

Hazel had been watching him off and on for the past half hour. It appeared that he was commanding her attention, without even knowing he had it. Then just as she came to the conclusion that he wasn't there to actually enjoy the women, a beautiful Dominican dancer sashayed over to him and proceeded to give him a lap dance. That's when she kicked herself for wishful thinking. He was no different than the rest of them. Maybe the dancer was someone special to him, a favorable stripper, something way beyond what others might assume. It kind of bothered her a little that she expected him to be different, and here he was feeling up on another bitch.

"What's on your mind?" said Mona, dropping down next to her on the sofa. She and Yvonnie had been receiving lap dances from dancers all evening, but it was all fun and laughs to them. Neither one of them were into women. They were not lesbians, just out to enjoy themselves.

"Why would you think something's on my mind?" she asked.

"You seemed distracted."

"That's because I am, sis," said Hazel.

"Okay. What is it?"

Hazel shrugged. "You see that nigga over there," she said and nodded in the direction of the person that had captured her undivided attention all evening. "The one in the green and white sweater, and white fitted cap."

"You talkin' about the nigga receivin' a lap dance from that Spanish chick, but not even payin' her no attention at all?" Mona replied, with a look of irritation on her face.

With those words, Hazel looked more closely now. To her astonishment, the guy did appear as though he had no interest in the dancer grinding herself upon his lap. More frankly, his attention was more on something else across the room from him. To someone with sharp observation, it was clear that he wasn't actually into the dancer, but more into watching something or someone else more attentively.

"He's not even stuck on her ass," Mona added.

"I see that now," said Hazel.

"Anyway, what's with him, sis?"

"I know him, Mona."

"From where?"

Again, Hazel shrugged. "I'm still trying to figure that part out right now," she said.

Then, all of a sudden, his gaze swung over to lock eyes with her. Hazel felt her breath catch, when they sat there looking at one another. He then reached up and tucked a twenty dollar bill into the dancer's G-string, before slapping her on the ass cheek. She rose up off him and strutted away.

"Your turn," Mona nudged her in the side.

"What?"

"Go over there and talk to him."

"Nah. I'm good."

Mona glanced over at Yvonnie and saw that she had two dancers on her lap now. She was slapping a stack of bills against their titties and laughing her ass off.

"Okay, now, you don't have to go to him because he's coming over here to you," said Mona.

Hazel was speechless as she watched the guy make his way over to her section. She couldn't take her eyes off of him. It was as though she was in a trance. Then, almost as if it was the natural thing to do, he sauntered over and slid down in the space between her and Mona. Hazel regarded him in silent wonder at his audacity.

"Do I know you?" asked Hazel.

"Your eyes say you do," he replied. "I'm Dee," he extended his hand in greeting.

"Hazel," she said hesitantly, but still took his hand.

"Once again, your eyes speaks a language of their own, and your name only compliments the essence of them. You look familiar, though. Where are you from?" he asked.

"I'm Brooklyn raised," she answered. "But for the past three years, I've been attending college, down in Georgia."

"Oh yeah? Which one?"

"Clark Atlanta."

Delani stroked his chin thoughtfully, and said, "Maybe that's where I remember those pretty brown eyes."

"You and your smooth words again," she said.

"I'm just speaking the truth, Hazel. I'm from Atlanta, as well, but then again, it's a big city."

"So what're you doing way up here in the Big Apple?"

"I've always wondered what New York is like, besides what I see in the movies and in music videos. So, it's the experience I'm really after, I guess. And so far, the view from here is…" Delani reached up to tuck a lock of her hair behind an ear. "Beautiful," he said.

Hazel blushed and batted her eyes dazzlingly.

"It's a small world," Mona interjected, and broke the spell between Hazel and him.

"But large enough to find my first diamond ever," said Delani.

From that point on, nothing else outside of the company they now shared existed, and he still had his eyes on his man. So did Marco and Wank Wank, for Hooliganz Crime Gang was in the building and back at it, again.

Chapter 30

Back in Harlem that same evening, Roxy stared over at Bizzy in agony and unbridled gratitude. She finally came to earlier, after being heavily sedated with shots of morphine, which he'd had delivered by Nurse Ranaja Brown, through Delani's influence. Leave it to Delani, he'd thought everything out before the mission was even completed. There were also some morphine tablets for Roxy, which she was popping like Skittles. She was in tremendous pain, but was pushing through it, like the champion she was.

Roxy had heard Bizzy and Youngin out, as they explained what they saw earlier. The two Hooliganz were just getting in through the front door, when they heard gun shots. Bizzy went out to investigate. When he recognized her, he convinced Youngin to help him help her. Together, they rescued her from the car and carried her inside. While Bizzy was tending to her wounds, Youngin, in disguise, went back out to try and remove the car from the scene, but quickly found out he couldn't. So, he left it where it was at, after ridding it of its illegalities, and headed back inside. Then, when Roxy told them why she was in the predicament she was in, both Youngin and Bizzy felt her pain. They then told her that they had recently just experienced something similar, back home.

"Where is back home?" she winced, with the sizzling Backwood in her hand, after taking a healthy pull from it.

Youngin said, "We're Southerners."

"Florida?" she said. "You guys are part of that Heathenz Crime Gang that broke out of prison recently?"

Roxy seemed very shocked by this, and both Hooliganz looked at one another in silent caution, in response to her statement. She knew exactly who they were.

"It's Hooliganz Crime Gang," Bizzy corrected her. "But I shouldn't have to tell you to keep…"

Roxy waved off whatever he was about to say in a painful gesture. "What's understood don't need to be explained, kid. But I must say, you guys are probably the most stupid muthafuckerz known to mankind," she said.

The disrespect made Youngin look at her crazily.

"What makes you say that, Roxy?" said Bizzy.

She hit the blunt again and passed it to Youngin, who accepted it without hesitation.

"You broke out of prison. Okay. But then you escaped to one of the three top states in the whole U.S. where fugitives run to, to hide and blend in. And New York is, by all means, the most common area where the Feds will be looking for you at. And here you are hanging out in Harlem, like you motherfuckerz are invisible or something. For someone to be clever enough to escape from prison, this move proves that you really aren't clever at all," Roxy said.

Once again, both Bizzy and Youngin exchanged a knowing look with one another.

"Don't mean to rain on your parade or anything."

"You made a very valid point, Roxy."

"Yet, I still can help you, if you'd allow me to," she said.

That really got Youngin's attention. "How?"

"I know a place far more convenient than a brownstone in Harlem, New York," Roxy pointed out agonizingly.

Bizzy nodded. "I'm listening."

"Is it really a dozen of you guys?"

"More," he said.

"How much more?"

After a brief pause to contemplate whether he should go through with dealing with Roxy, by entrusting her with the family's business, Youngin gave her the total count. She was blown away by the number, but still said she could make it happen.

"Make it happen how, Roxy?"

"You'll see," she replied. "But first, I'm gonna need your help with something."

"What's that?" said Bizzy.

"I need a lift to my own place, so I can show you what I have in mind," she said.

"And you sure that's wise wit' your situation?"

Roxy popped another morphine tablet into her mouth. "Nobody knows where I actually live, Bizzy."

"Yeah, right."

"I'll bet my life on it," she exclaimed.

Looking down at the time on his watch, Youngin saw that it was several minutes past six, which meant that night time was near, and that would be their next movement period.

"Until then," said Bizzy, he told her to brace herself for a dressing change of her wound.

Her bandages were leaking through with blood, and he almost was tempted to taker her over to the Harlem Hospital nearby.

"I have a cousin, who works as a registered nurse at the Harlem Hospital," Roxy said, as if reading his mind. "I think I need to give her a call."

"I think you should, too," said Youngin in a serious tone.

"How about now?" Bizzy suggested.

She thought about it for a second. "Bring me my phone then."

Thirty minutes later, the Hooliganz were parked outside the hospital, after dropping Roxy off there, a minute ago. They were on alert for any sign of the law, or that crazy ass nigga, Hood, out there lurking.

Roxy appreciated Bizzy's help and all that he did for her, but she needed to make sure her shit was properly examined and handled by a real doctor. In case of probing questions that she knew would be coming, upon her inpatient status, Roxy had already devised a believable story to go with. She didn't have to be told that the authorities would be informed about the situation. The cousin, Kim, who was the head nurse on shift, was in good with the big man of the house and was assigned Roxy's appointed caregiver. She would play her part accordingly.

"What you think, B?" asked Youngin. He was very watchful and privy to the seriousness of the matter.

"Apparently, she knows what she's talking about."

"Do you trust her?" he asked.

"I'm pretty sure the trust line had already been drawn, Youngin."

"Yeah. I trust her enough to reveal what she knows, where we can determine our own game plan."

"We'll see."

Bizzy nodded. "We damn sure will."

Chapter 31

It wasn't until the next morning that Delani received the disturbing phone call from White Boy Ty about his mother. The house was quiet as a mouse, until he screamed in an outrage. That sent Dejah and Shamar, and a few others, rushing to his bedroom, at once. Shamar was the first to arrive, and he found his brother in great distress.

By midmorning, the whole team knew what was going on, and now something must be done about it. Delani wanted both former Royals to pay for what they did. Princess and Naomi both were now living on borrowed time. It was bad enough that Toby had to turn herself in to the authorities, and now this shit. The incident went down hours after it was known that Kiara would get off on the murders. Being that Toby was now in the building, there was no question what she was planning to do about it. With the other Royals locked up in the county, besides Princess and Naomi, and now, Toby, it was a lot of pressure in the air. Shit was about to go down.

Meanwhile, Delani had been hit with another situation, regarding Bizzy and Youngin's bullshit. When Rikah brought the matter to his attention, he was instantly shocked by it. He demanded their presence, and sent a team of Hooliganz over to retrieve Bizzy and Youngin. Then, when he got the call that neither one of them were at their Harlem brownstone apartment, that's all it took for Delani to have dark thoughts.

"Find out who this bitch, Roxy, is and where we can find her," replied Dejah solemnly, seeing the murderous rage in Delani's eyes towards the situation.

Rikah nodded and went to go do just that.

"The hell them niggaz got going on? They tryna get us fucked up or something?" Delani said, gazing up at a frustrated looking Dejah from his squat position.

"Maybe they know something we don't know, Dee. We both know Bizzy ain't no dumb nigga, little brotha. But for him to pull a stunt like that, he has to know something. Something that he feel could benefit the family," LJ spoke up.

Delani did not even acknowledge him. Delani was still mad about how the situation went between LJ and Shamar, the other night. To hear that LJ beat Shamar and put him in the trunk of a car made him bitter. Delani wanted to fight him about that, but left the situation alone, seeing how LJ and Shamar had obviously made up.

"Unfortunately, as crazy as that sounds, I gotta say that what LJ said is true," said Dejah. "Bizzy ain't no dumb nigga, and he always plottin' on something."

"Like somebody else we know," smirked Chili Willie, the quiet but dangerous Hooligan, who lived out back in the pool house, which he'd claimed as his own. He and Booby were roommates, two thoroughbred shooters, and their presence around the house was worthwhile.

Right then, the front door opened, and Rikah announced that Bizzy and Youngin both were pulling up now.

"Mothufuckaz," muttered Delani, before marching towards the door.

"Dee?" Dejah called out after him.

He looked back at her.

"Be cool. Hear what they have to say, first," she said. Dejah could plainly see that he was about to flip out.

Minutes later, Bizzy, Rikah, Youngin and Shoo Baby entered the mansion, and were led into the large family room.

"Before you snap on us," said Bizzy, when he walked into the room and saw the grave look on Delani's face.

The head honcho himself was sitting on the arm of the sofa, lighting up his third blunt of the day.

"I have something to say," he replied.

Delani didn't even respond to him. So, Bizzy went into his explanation anyway, and didn't hold nothing back. In the process, Youngin added a little in, here and there, along the way. The focal point was Roxy Morgan and what she was able to do to help the HCG crew.

It was shared that Roxy was a known killer and hustler, with major connections. She was also the niece of a big time music producer, who was connected to Jay-Z, and even rapper Cam'ron. She was in the loop and took hits for hire. Roxy knew people who knew people. That led Bizzy and Youngin just up the street from where they stood now, where another mansion and another hideaway was available to accommodate the crew. The homes belonged to her people, whom Roxy assured them that they were hers to have, and for Hooliganz Crime Gang to utilize, at their own leisure.

"Sounds like she's a charm," said Dejah. She was definitely looking forward to meeting her.

"She said her people let her borrow the homes to lay low, whenever she needed a place to duck off," said Bizzy.

"And what did you say the name was of the nigga, who tried to slump the bitch?" asked LJ.

"Hood," Bizzy said.

"His real name, brah." LJ seemed really anxious by this.

Youngin was the one who answered next. "His name is Keith Thompson, or something like that."

"Thompson," said LJ. "That's that nigga name."

"Yeah. How you know, LJ?"

"Because," LJ replied, then he swiveled his eyes over at Delani in surprise. "Remember the lawyer chick I told you I met at the Hudson, the other night?"

"Please don't tell me this Hood nigga is the same muthafucka your chick helped beat that case?" said Dejah.

LJ nodded. "Yep."

"Damn," Delani dropped his head for a moment, and let out an exasperating breath. "One muthafuckin' problem after another, and we ain't even got fully settled up this bitch yet. We already fuckin' up, early in the game," he said.

A moment of silence hung in the air.

"Hmph." Dejah folded her arms with a smirk on her face. "I see everybody's meeting New York's finest of the crops now, huh?"

"What're you talkin' about, Dej?" said Bizzy.

"Ask Dee what I'm talkin' about," she shot back at him.

Delani scowled in her direction.

Shoo baby walked passed Delani and ran a hand over his wavy hair.

"You niggas and these funny talkin' bitches," she said, and went towards the kitchen area.

"What's up wit' that shit, my nigga?" said Youngin.

"Nothin," he said.

Then he got up and walked out the room to go be by himself. He needed some space to think, and some fresh air to breathe.

Out back, near the big infinity pool, is where the iPhone buzzed in his front pocket. He fished it out and glanced down at the screen to see who it was. It was hazel. His cold heart leapt with joy at the prospect of hearing her voice again.

"You miss me already?" Delani answered.

A short giggle came over the phone. "What if I told you that I am missing you already? I had a great time last night at the club with you."

"Likewise."

"What're you doing tonight?"

"Do you really wanna know what I'll be doing?"
She said, "Yes."
Delani grinned broadly. "Tonight, I will be in the company of the most beautiful brown eyes in humanity, while eating somethin' Italian and drinkin' somethin' I can't pronounce."

That made her laugh. He did, too. And that was all it took to humble that monster in him that was anxiously begging to be released. It was Hazel. Those eyes were magical. Spellbound.

Chapter 32

To have influence could be both a gift and a curse, but at that moment, for Toby, it was a blessing to still have influence, in spite of the odds stacked against her. It took not even 48 hours for Toby to gain dominion in her new environment. Of the five Royals that were in the housing unit, three of them were considered the enemy, while Toby took the other two and established order within their living quarters. The other women, who were not affiliated but acknowledged, were glad Toby had shown up and started regulating things.

Prior to her arrival, it was India, who had been calling all the shots. It was India, who ordered Princess and Naomi to do what they did to Kiara. Unfortunately for them, they had been rehoused up front on the 6x9 confinement cell. They were now roommates, and about to be very miserable, once Toby had gotten to ahold of them.

The only two who had been keeping it real was Myrikal and Sasha Blac. Before Toby got there, they were already planning to crush India and the others. But when Toby walked through the door in the unit and learned that India was the bitch in charge, she put a stop to that quick. She broke that bitch's jaw, and made Myrikal and Sasha Blac beat that hoe to sleep. Then they got on Jayda and Reyneshia's asses, and made them check out of the unit. Only three Royals remained, Toby, the ruler, and both Sasha Blac and Myrikal, the two enforcers.

The women's housing unit was a big open bay area. There were no cells, like it was in Leon County jail, and nowhere for anyone to run and hide, when the smoke is up. There was no privacy whatsoever. It was a jungle in there.

By the 8th day, Toby had utilized her influence to get Kiara back into the unit with them. She had been the victim. Therefore, she was still eligible to be housed in general population. Toby felt she could do more for Kiara, if she was back on the unit. She could protect her, and it would make Kiara happy to be amongst real family. Thanks to Jeremy's auntie, Carole, who was the captain of the jailhouse and a good friend to Kiara, she made it all possible. She knew by reputation what Toby was capable of, and knew Kiara would be in safe hands.

Now that she was back in the unit, Kiara and Toby shared and appreciated one another's company. Seeing Delani and Vermani's mother in the condition she was in made her boil inside with murderous rage. They had messed the poor woman's face up so bad, she had to get over eighty stitches. Her jaw, too, was broken, and Kiara was in a lot of pain. Her condition complicated things, but Toby saw to it that everything got done. The woman was so very saddened. If Toby had seen Kiara prior to doing what she did to the other former Royals, no doubt, someone would be dead. However, though, their time was coming, and when it did come, it was going to be ugly.

On the 11th day, Toby was called out for a visit, and found Jamir and Harmoni waiting for her. Beside them, on the other side of the thick, scarred Plexiglas window, was Harold, Monica, and Uncle Bart. They were there to see Kiara, and had a rude awakening coming. Bart reached over to put his palm against the glass, and Toby did the same.

"How you doing?" said Jamir.

He was glowing on the outside, fresh shape up, and hood fresh, as usual.

Toby sighed, "I'm maintaining, lil brah."

"And Mama Kay?"

"Heartbreaking," said Toby. "You about to see her in a minute. It don't look good. But overall, we good. I got Sasha Blac and Myrikal back there wit' me."

Jamir said, "That's good. You got a solid team. Big brotha and 'em asked about you. It's wild out here, but you know nothin' don't faze HCG. The gang is good, sis."

"What's up wit' that lawyer though?"

"His name is Terry Stutson. He worked wit' Mama Kay's lawyer and he's a beast. He'll be pullin' up on you real soon, my nigga," said Jamir. Then he paused for a moment and Toby recognized the sadness spread over his face.

Harmoni took the phone away from him and she and Toby talked for a minute. That was until Kiara rolled up in the room, and all hell broke loose on the other side of the glass. When Harold saw his wife, he damn near hit the roof. Monica was beside herself with anger and sadness. Kiara kept her head high and refused to let them see her sweat. Harold had to humble himself. Good thing Uncle Bart was there to calm him down. The man was trying to bang his way through the glass window to get to her.

"My God," was all Harmoni could say, when she laid eyes on Kiara, in the wheelchair.

"Don't worry about me," said Kiara in a strong voice, next to Toby. "Toby got me in here. She's been amazing," she said, through the pain in her broken jaw.

She couldn't even open her mouth to actually talk, like normal people. From next to her, Toby reached over and laid a hand upon Kiara's shoulder. For the next hour, the visitation room was filled with love and anguish. By the time they made it back to the unit, Toby was emotionally exhausted. She laid down, threw an arm over her eyes, and sunk into her own quiet self-pity. She missed White Boy Ty. She missed the streets. Most of all, she missed her period, and that was fucking with her the most. Toby was scared out of her mind. She was pregnant. Before she even realized it,

Toby had fallen into a fitful sleep, while her people watched over her, but that wasn't about to be her worst mistake. It was putting her trust in the enemy, whose hands her life would be in, one she would least expect to do her in, the total unexpected.

Chapter 33

Duke, Bred Man, Mane, Taquan and Rod finally came home from their little bid in the Tent, over in Tallahassee. These were the Junior Hooliganz, the youngest of the youngest, and the most vicious ones in the crew. They were the ones who had the most to prove, willing to do whatever it took to earn their stripes. The youngest was Mane. At thirteen years old, he was by far the meanest little muthafucker that Delani ever had the pleasure of recruiting.

Then there was Duke, Rod and Bred Man, all fourteen and their young legacy was reputable with violence and hustling, the true epitome of go-getters. The Feds couldn't hold them and were forced to honor their release. But it was fifteen year old Taquan, who emerged from the Tent on some other shit. He was both mad and petrified over what he knew was about to become of him now. Taquan was on a mission and nothing else mattered.

The HCG crew threw a block party for their youngsters, and everybody showed up to welcome them home. It was a big event in Pepper Hill, over at the Steven School Park, and all the way over to Black Top Pool. The homecoming of the Junior Hooliganz brought the whole hood out. It was a movie. Tilly and White Boy Ty welcomed their baby brothers home, in class and style.

While everybody celebrated, Taquan found his way over to DaJhana's house, where everything was about to change. When he made it to the front door and knocked, Tiwanna had answered it. At the sight of her, he felt his heart skip a beat, with a surge of excitement.

"Taquan," she was astounded.

Without a word, he stepped forward and wrapped his arms around her. He had been anticipating this moment, when he heard about what went down. When he got the news, Taquan was angered and ready to crush something.

"It's good to have you back home," said Tiwanna, rubbing a hand over his back, in a soothing gesture. "C'mon in the house, baby boy," she told him.

Taquan entered the house and Tiwanna shut the door behind him. Upon entry, he noticed that the house was strangely quiet, but it still beheld that scent of lemon Pine Sol and scented candles that he remembered.

The story behind the connection was created from Tiwanna and Taquan's big brother Jason's relationship, before Jason went off to prison two years ago, but Tiwanna's love for Taquan remained unmoved. She became the big sister that he never had. In the process, the budding friendship between Taquan and DaJhana became a relationship that was earned, and Taquan made her his first love. He even had to battle Broozy to earn his respect and his right to be in his little sister's life, as her boyfriend. That was his sole reason for being there, to check up on DaJhana and resume his love and loyalty to her. He'd endured many sleepless nights, stressing over his girlfriend and the obstacles she was forced to go through.

"Where is Daj?" he asked.

"In her bedroom," she answered.

Taquan hesitated.

"Go." Tiwanna graced a manicured hand over his nappy fro. "Don't be scared, Taquan. I'm sure she will be happy to see you," she whispered.

Taquan heard her clearly, but the sadness he saw in her eyes was just as obvious.

"I'll be back to check up on you," he said.

"Don't worry about me, baby boy."

Taquan nodded. "Say what you wanna but I'm sorry I wasn't here to…"

"Go!" Tiwanna pointed towards the hallway. "I don't want to hear that foolishness. Go to your girl, Taquan."

With a deep sigh, Taquan did as he was told and made his way to DaJhana's bedroom. The door was ajar, and he could hear the sounds of Jhene Aiko's *Frequency* playing at a low volume from inside. Taquan slowly pushed the door wider and saw DaJhana asleep in her bed. Taquan paused, just inside her bedroom door, staring in on her and growing anxious by the second. Then he entered the room, walked over to her bed, and eased down upon it. The instant his weight sunk down onto the bed, DaJhana's eyes slowly fluttered opened. She had been laying on her side, almost in a fetal position, with her face upon her hand. Her eyes traveled up at him and she stared at him for a second. Then, suddenly, DaJhana was bolting up in bed.

"Taquan?" she said in disbelief.

"In the flesh," he grinned.

She gasped, threw her arms around him, and squeezed him lovingly in her embrace. Then she cried for all it was worth to him and her both. Taquan figured this was going to happen, and had already prepared himself for it.

"I needed you so bad, Quan," she cried.

"I know," Taquan held her.

Her tears came nonstop, and Taquan didn't dare let her go. He felt her pain and empathized with her because he was no stranger to death and loss. He too lost his baby brother, Nario, when he was eleven. Nario was only eight years old, when he ran in the street and got run over by a car. Taquan had witnessed the whole thing and that was where his violent mentality had derived from. Ever since Nario's death, he had not been the same joyous, innocent boy he once was. Taquan's pain and hatred accounted for his troublesome demeanor. He was traumatized.

After DaJhana's cries subsided, long enough for her to tell him what she'd been through without him, Taquan listened with a heavy heart. He already knew the incident was due to some personal shit between Baby Gal and her little brother, Corey. He was well aware of who Corey was, for they had a long history of competing for DaJhana's love. They used to really go at it over her, and DaJhana was overwhelmed by the attention. What sixteen year old girl wouldn't be? It was also understood that she liked them both, but it was Taquan who she really wanted the most.

"Now all I got is Tiwanna," DaJhana replied

"And me, too," he said.

She nodded.

When he was about to say something, she caught her breath in alertness. Then she took him by the hand and pulled him over across the hall, into Broozy's room.

"What's up?" said Taquan.

"I found something I know you'll prolly have some use for now that Broozy…"

"Don't say it," he put a finger to her lips. "Just show me what you got," said Taquan.

She nodded, then went over to the bedroom closet and snatched the door opened.

"I was waiting until you come home to show you," DaJhana replied hurriedly.

She stepped into the closet and moved things around for a minute, before she emerged. In her hands, DaJhana was holding a Nike shoe box and a backpack. She told him about having avoided coming into Broozy's bedroom, for fear of the energy it would bring. Then she threw caution to the wind and went inside anyway. She found what she got, after cleaning up his bedroom, knowing Broozy had risked his life and freedom.

Taquan said, "Lemme hold the bag."

He heard the familiar sound of guns clanking around in the backpack. She didn't want it in her possession any more than he cared for her to have it. Sure enough, it was Broozy's arsenal inside the back pack. Two Glocks, a Ruger, an Uzi machine gun, and even a sawed-off .12 Guage shotgun. Included in the backpack was a ski mask, gloves, a blue bandana, a flat head screwdriver, and some duct tape.

"Here," DaJhana presented the shoe box.

Inside the box was a thousand pills contained in a Ziploc bag, a quarter brick of heroin, two ounces of coke, some weed, and three bundles of cash. Taquan handed her the money and said, "I'll take the rest and make it happen."

"How much is it?" she asked.

"Count it and see."

DaJhana stared at the money in her hand.

"Use it to take care the house and make sure you do it wisely."

"I know, Quan." DaJhana bumped shoulders with him, and he nodded.

"What about Souljah, though?" she asked.

"What about him?"

When she told him about Souljah confronting her about what her brother owed him from the last mission they were on, Taquan automatically knew it was bullshit. He knew Souljah and he was glad she didn't fall for that shit.

"When the last time you saw him?"

"Yesterday," she said.

He frowned. "A'ight. I'll take care of Souljah."

"Don't get in no trouble, bae."

"I won't," he promised.

She didn't believe him. Taquan was about to confront Souljah, and that could only go two ways, neither was good.

Chapter 34

Amelia Graham had just made it back to her office at Graham & Blackmun Law Firm, when her personal assistant had paged her service phone atop her desk.

"There's a Mr. November here for you," she said.

"Mr. November?" said Amelia with puzzlement. Then it suddenly registered who exactly this Mr. November was. The thought of LJ showing up unexpectedly at her workplace would be regarded as unacceptable without an appointment, if it was someone else, but she was delighted to see him.

"Send him in," Amelia replied.

"Will do," her personal assistant said.

A minute later, LJ entered the spacious office, carrying a picnic basket in his hand and a smirk on his face. Amelia looked up at the young, good-looking Hooligan and her pussy automatically became damp. She couldn't get enough of his young thug love, and he pleased her well.

"What is this?" she stood up behind her desk.

"A picnic," answered LJ.

"In my office, though?" she replied.

He nodded.

"How corny," she laughed, and he frowned. "But I love it. It's so spontaneous of you."

"Surprised?"

"Very much so, and I'm famished."

LJ locked the door, and she paged her assistant to tell her to hold all phone calls and clear her schedule for the next hour. She was about to take her much needed break and enjoy the quality time with her young Hooligan. Amelia could just about imagine what was going through her colleagues' minds at that point. It was one thing she had represented the very same criminal she had fallen for, but here she was now courting a younger black man, and seemed to be enjoying this new relationship. She didn't give a fuck what others thought of her, and she damn well couldn't care less what they thought of LJ. He was risking everything to give her happiness.

After hugging and kissing him welcomingly, LJ then spread out the big fluffy beach blanket over the floor of the office. She then awakened the music app on her laptop and put on some jazz music. Then she sat down across from LJ, as he set out tuna fish and cold cut sandwiches, grapes, Lays potato chips, chocolate chip cookies, and a bottle of chilled champagne. The bottle of champagne astounded her, and Amelia was very impressed with his efforts.

"This is the first time this has happened," she said.

"But not the last."

"I hope not," she said. "I love it, honey."

He leaned in and kissed her lips. "That's why I do it."

"But why am I beginning to believe that this visit is more than just a lunch date?"

"Because it's not just a lunch date, Amelia," he admitted to her. "Let's eat and small talk first," said LJ.

Reluctantly, they begin to eat their food, while LJ asked how her day was going so far. The life of a criminal attorney was a challenging thing, but it was fulfilling in a way that many people would not understand. In exchange, LJ told her about his plans to invest in something worthwhile and lucrative enough to be happy with.

"And what's your interests?"

"I have a few things in mind," said LJ.

"Such as?"

"Whatever fifty grand would grant me in the form of being a profitable investor. I was thinking about something along the lines of fashion and agriculture," he said.

"Fashion and agriculture?" her eyebrows raised.

"Something like that," said LJ.

"That sounds intriguing, Leonardo. You might have your work cut out for you with that one, which I'm sure, if you put your brilliant mind to it, you'll succeed."

Okay, she was tired of the small talk and wanted LJ to get to the meat of the matter, for which he had really come. He noticed this and could tell she was anxious for him to tell her the real deal.

"Where can I find Keith Thompson?" he asked. The question instantly made her stiffen with alertness.

"Why are you asking me this?"

"You still wish for him to be punished, right?"

It took her a long time to respond, and when she did, it was not what he expected to hear.

"I forgave him already, Leonardo," she said.

"You forgave him?"

She nodded. "Yes."

"And when did you manage to do this?"

"About a week ago."

"In person?"

"No. I mean, not exactly. It was during communion at mass, when I found it in my heart to forgive that bastard of a man. Then he called my phone, two days later, on Facetime, and that's when it happened."

"You forgave him?"

She chuckled.

"You make is sound so… censorious."

"I don't even know what that shit means, but it's all good, though. I guess it doesn't matter anymore."

"What doesn't matter?" she asked, sensing something grave was about to transpire between them.

"Forget about it, Amelia."

"No," she said briskly. "Tell me, honey. I need to know what's on your mind. What is it?"

"Us," said LJ. "I can't make a happier life wit' you wit' him still in the picture."

"He's not in the picture of my life anymore, Leonardo. Keith is now just a chapter of my past."

LJ gave her a hard look that made her uneasy.

"Then how about explaining to me why this picture even exists," he replied, before materializing his cell phone and pecking away at the screen. Then he extended the phone out towards her, and she took it hesitantly.

When Amelia gazed down at the phone, she brought a hand up to her mouth at what she saw. It was a picture of, none other than, Keith "Hood" Thompson himself, standing outside her building, dressed in all black. The pose in which he presented was and could be described as suspicious, as if waiting to do something very drastic or something. Amelia gauged his facial expression, and also knew that look well. It was a look that always ended with him doing something extremely bad.

"When was this taken, Leonardo?" She finally found her voice, after the shock.

"Just now, when I was coming in to see you. Maybe he was waiting for you to come outside, or something," said LJ. "But before I let anything happen to you, I'll take care of it my damn self."

"But why would anything happen to me? I didn't do anything to deserve…"

"Guilty by association," he cut her off.

"Guilty by…" Amelia had to catch herself. "That's the most ridiculous hogwash I've ever heard," she said.

"Look, Amelia. Your association wit' this nigga is likely to place you in danger. There's some very bad people out here lookin' for him for what they believe he's guilty of."

"The murder?" she said.

He nodded. "And just as soon as they get wind that you two had anything going on, they'll come after you to get to him. Qaydon Miller was a powerful figure in the streets, and his death meant a lot to some people, enough to seek revenge, even if it means hurtin' you in the process."

Amelia looked horrified.

To convince her to see things his way, LJ knew he had to give it to her blood raw, without giving himself up. But the nigga, Hood, was really out there lurking, and LJ wanted to do something about it, for the sake of Amelia's safety, and her family's as well, but most of all, for the sake of Roxy's vengeance and her now being a great asset to his organization. She was the mission. Give her what could be given on Hood, and in exchange, she would provide the goods on what she knew on such matters that would benefit HCG. That was the game plan, to use Amelia to get to Hood and give him to Roxy, in exchange for insurance.

"I will tell you everything," said Amelia.

"You sure?"

She nodded.

"You'll protect me, right?"

"That's what I'm here for, baby," said LJ seriously.

Amelia sighed miserably. "So much for a lunch date and a wonderful picnic," she muttered.

Chapter 35

Sasha Blac gazed at Toby as she turned over on her side during her sleep. She was braiding Kiara's hair and telling her all about her goals in life. Meanwhile, Myrikal was on the wall phone, engaged in conversation with her loved ones. Neither of them had a clue as to the atrocities that were about to take place, but Charmaine Butler did because it was her, who was about to initiate the whole incident.

It was by eavesdropping on the Royals conversations that Charmaine learned the identity of who the actual person was that murdered her son, Jarvis, recently. Those two dumb bitches, India and Naomi, were literally trading war stories, without being observant or wise, and had given up Toby's name as the killer. For two months now, since Jarvis' murder, his killer was all Charmaine could think about. She had heard it through the grapevine that her son was allegedly killed by a female, but the name never was revealed. It was also said that Royal Mafia was behind the death of her son.

When the Royals came to jail recently, it was then that Charmaine considered confronting them about it. But then her conscience told her to be still and wait it out. Plus, she was too outnumbered anyway to try and do something about it. She wanted the actual killer that took her son away. And here Toby was, having practically fallen into her muthafuckin' lap.

Prior to Toby's arrival, Charmaine had manipulated her way into the Royals' trust by cleaning up behind them, making their beds, hand washing their clothes. She was no stranger to such things. That was her hustle and how she ate, when she could. Charmaine played them bitches close. Through all the heartache and humiliation she had to endure, her efforts paid off with the closeness of the very same bitch responsible for killing her only child. There would be nothing or no one holding her back now.

Toby was in her sight now, and it was only right that she take advantage of this opportunity. She'd been patient far too long now. It was crunch time, and Charmaine, who was bunked next to Toby's bunk, which was on the top, over Kiara bunk, was more than pleased by the action she was about to take.

As she sat down on her bottom bunk, sneaking glances up at Toby, as she slept, Charmaine eased her shank out from the hole in her pillow. She did it so discreetly that no one was the wiser to what she was doing. In all her forty-six years of living and being a well-known dope smoker and thief, Charmaine had done her share of bad things to people, along the way. In the shadows, she'd done a lot of wicked things that she wasn't proud of. It was all a survival thing to her. She had to do what she had to do. She had prepared herself for this moment, the moment where nothing mattered except to avenge Jarvis's death.

Charmaine clutched the handle of the shank and rose up to her feet. Toby's back was toward her, as she stood between the bunks. She glanced over at Sasha Blac, who was standing behind Kiara, and working on her last two braids. Across the unit, Myrikal was no longer on the phone, but walking towards the TV area.

Charmaine took a deep breath and reached up to shake Toby's shoulder. Toby woke up and turned over to look at her. Charmaine upped the shank and stabbed Toby in the left eye socket with it. She withdrew the shank and repeatedly begin to plunge the shank into her face, chest area, and neck, until Sasha Blac football tackled her to the floor between the beds, and she became the victim next.

"No," Kiara cried out, and went to Toby, who had fallen from the top bunk onto the floor.

Myrikal rushed over at once, and together, she and Sasha Blac fought against Charmaine's wrath.

"Somebody call for help," shouted one of the other women present to witness the incident.

Two other women began kicking and shouting on the entrance door of the unit to get the guard's attention. By this time, Toby was bleeding furiously as her eyeball hung out of its socket. She was coughing up blood, and even her arm was bent in an awkward angle, resulting from her fall.

Kiara ignored her own pain and agony and cradled Toby's head in her lap as she struggled to fight the threat of death trying to claim her life. When the officials came, the business was already done to Charmaine, and yet Myrikal was still stabbing away at her lifeless body, in a dark rage.

Toby was loaded onto a stretcher and rushed out immediately, so was Sasha Blac, who could still walk but not without leaving a trail of blood in her wake. The unit had become a bloody site for all. It was a crime scene, and Myrikal didn't stop hacking away at Charmaine until a high level of voltage from a guard's taser gun hit her and had her doing the Harlem shake. She was cuffed and dragged away from the dead body.

Kiara was in a panic and didn't know what to do, so she went for her own shank that Toby had made for her. Then she stole away Sasha Blac's knife, as well, arming herself to put in some work, in case a bitch tried their luck on her, too. That was until her old friend Camilla Brooks had come over to take her side. This was another well-known crackhead, who was just as dangerous as she was a woman. She and Kiara held their own, and dared anyone to test them.

Seeing what was done to Toby made Kiara realize how alert and vicious she needed to be now. Toby was caught lacking, and had paid a severe price for it. She might not make it out of this one. It was a cold world they were living in, and even the coldest muthafucker should be aware of the treacherousness of the world. Shit just got real, and it was about to get even realer.

Chapter 36

It was past three o'clock that afternoon, before White Boy Ty, fortified by a nice fat blunt of Kush and a bottle of Fruitopia, went back inside the hospital. He was out with Marco, Kweli and the Junior Hooliganz, when the call came about Toby. Kiara had reached out to Harold, and Harold called Monica, who immediately called Ty to tell him what went down. He hurried straight for the Quincy hospital and violated all traffic laws to get there.

Toby had been stabbed twelve times and lost an eye in the process. She'd also lost a considerable amount of blood and her pride, all at the same time. During her rush to the hospital, she had flat-lined twice, but the paramedics brought her back both times. Ty confronted the two paramedics responsible of saving her life, and they told him everything. That day was the first time the Hooliganz ever saw him cry.

The surgery was still ongoing, after two hours of working to at least attempt to repair Toby's existence. She had three doctors in there working to save what was left of her. It was a very sobering experience. Toby was in bad shape. White Boy Ty hated the fact that three police officers were parked outside the operating room. He knew there wasn't a snowball chance in hell that Toby would be going without being heavily guarded. She was still considered under custody of the law, and now labeled critical.

Once again, Royal Mafia and the HCG crew were prowling the hallways of the hospital, like before, but this time they came together as one unit, one whole, and their unity was shaped by their love and loyalty to Toby. Tilly was going crazy.

"I knew some shit like this would happen," said White Boy Ty in a breath of disgruntlement.

Zamon looked over at him and said, "What you mean, you knew it would happen?"

"I knew somethin' was gonna go wrong, if I let her outta my sight," said Ty.

"Well, you did, and look what happened," Zamon muttered.

Ty glared at him darkly. The look Jamir saw in his eyes made him toss an arm over White Boy Ty's shoulder and pull him back towards the exit. He shot Zamon a hard look, in turn, and Lil Eddie slapped him in the back of the head in contempt.

"I don't need no muthafuckin' hand holdin' Jay," said Ty, as they neared the exit door.

"Just come wit' me back outside, brah. We can't do shit for Toby right now."

"I can do somethin' for her."

"What? Other than feel sorry for her and kick yourself over some bullshit that was outta your control? C'mon, big brah, don't let this shit faze you."

They made it outside to Jamir's car, where they got inside and another Backwood was fired up. Blowing some good bud was damn near the medicine to all emotional despair. Although he knew White Boy Ty had just come from outside burning one, Jamir felt he needed another one, and this time with the likes of himself present.

Then he got the phone call from his new acquaintance by the name of Nyaisha. She was demanding his presence, saying she had something interesting to show him. When Jamir told her what was going on and where he was, Nyaisha insisted that she would rather meet him there instead.

"Is it that important?" he asked.

"Yes," she said.

With an exasperating breath, Jamir said, "Pull up then, I'll be outside. Just try and make it short because I'm in the middle of somethin' right now."

"I already know, Jamir. I'm on my way."

"A'ight."

After disconnecting with her, Jamir gazed over at Ty and saw silent tears rolling down his face. This was shocking to Jamir because he had never seen this before. That's how he knew his feelings were for real, when it came to Toby.

"She gon' be good, my nigga. Stop crying," said Jamir.

Right at that moment, White Boy Ty said, "She was pregnant, lil brah. That's what the fuck is bothering me."

"What? Pregnant?"

"She told me two nights ago. Now I don't know if that shit done fucked it up or not," Ty stressed.

Jamir didn't know what to say. All he did was reach over and grab his brothaz hand. Sometimes all it took was a hand held to bring comfort to one's heart. Hearing that Toby was pregnant really blew Jamir's mind, as he took the blunt and pulled on it hard. He needed to smoke to that unexpected revelation. Toby being with child was the last thing anybody would expect, given her reputation and gangsta lifestyle. That was scary in itself.

Minutes later, Nyaisha arrived in the same car she had been in recently at the Chinese restaurant. She texted Jamir's phone to inform him of her arrival. Then the car pulled up behind the McLaren F1 and parked in the road, at the rear of Jamir's car.

"Just chill, my nigga. I'll be right back," said Jamir.

Then he opened up the door and got out of the car. Ty remained seated, while puffing on his blunt to ease his mind from the wicked thoughts that consumed him. As he gazed outside around him, White Boy Ty saw five of his Hooliganz posted up outside the building. They were there to watch Jamir's back, as always. If only Toby had that kind of security around her, then maybe he wouldn't be there right now, thought Ty, as he felt another tear threaten to slip out. That was when he peered into the rearview mirror, and something gave him pause. He leaned in closer to the mirror, then looked behind him at the person Jamir was now standing outside with. When he recognized who it was, his heart and his mouth dropped. Immediately, Ty was out of the car and moving in her and Jamir's direction.

"Shamoorah?" he called out.

Instantly, the female standing before Jamir looked up at his voice and saw White Boy Ty coming towards her. Then he gripped her around the neck, slammed her back against the car, and put his pistol to her head.

Jamir panicked. "Brah, what you doing?"

Sneering darkly in the face of the bitch whom he dreamed of murdering one day, White Boy Ty said, "The fuck you got going on, Shamoorah?"

She was so scared, it left her speechless.

"Shamoorah?" said Jamir, with confusion on his face. "I think you're mistaken, big brah."

"Am I?" said Ty, squeezing her throat harder and watching as her eyes popped out in fear. Her face was so red, as she struggled to breathe under his pressure.

Them Hooliganz came running, and that was when the sounds of a child crying came from the backseat. When Ty risked glancing in its direction, he saw a little girl sitting in a car seat in the back. She was looking out the window at him and crying her poor little heart out. It was at that very moment that everything changed for White Boy Ty. What he saw in that little girl's eyes was the very same blue eyes he saw when he looked into the mirror. Shamoorah had unexpectedly surfaced, and with her, she brought a truth so profound it paralyzed him. The little girl was a spitting image of him. It was scary.

To be continued…

Lock Down Publications and Ca$h Presents Assisted Publishing Packages

BASIC PACKAGE $499 Editing Cover Design Formatting	UPGRADED PACKAGE $800 Typing Editing Cover Design Formatting
ADVANCE PACKAGE $1,200 Typing Editing Cover Design Formatting Copyright registration Proofreading Upload book to Amazon	LDP SUPREME PACKAGE $1,500 Typing Editing Cover Design Formatting Copyright registration Proofreading Set up Amazon account Upload book to Amazon Advertise on LDP, Amazon and Facebook Page

***Other services available upon request.
Additional charges may apply

Lock Down Publications
P.O. Box 944
Stockbridge, GA 30281-9998
Phone: 470 303-9761

Submission Guideline

Submit the first three chapters of your completed manuscript to ldpsubmissions@gmail.com. In the subject line add **Your Book's Title**. The manuscript must be in a Word Doc file and sent as an attachment. Document should be in Times New Roman, double spaced, and in size 12 font. Also, provide your synopsis and full contact information. If sending multiple submissions, they must each be in a separate email.

Have a story but no way to send it electronically? You can still submit to LDP/Ca$h Presents. Send in the first three chapters, written or typed, of your completed manuscript to:

LDP: Submissions Dept
P.O. Box 944
Stockbridge, GA 30281-9998

DO NOT send original manuscript. Must be a duplicate.
Provide your synopsis and a cover letter containing your full contact information.

Thanks for considering LDP and Ca$h Presents.

NEW RELEASES

BLOODLINE OF A SAVAGE 1&2
THESE VICIOUS STREETS
RELENTLESS GOON
RELENTLESS GOON 2
BY PRINCE A. TAUHID

THE BUTTERFLY MAFIA 1-3
BY FUMIYA PAYNE

A THUG'S STREET PRINCESS 1&2
BY MEESHA

CITY OF SMOKE 2
BY MOLOTTI

STEPPERS 1,2&3
BY KING RIO

THE LANE 1&2
BY KEN-KEN SPENCE

THUG OF SPADES 1&2
LOVE IN THE TRENCHES 2
BY COREY ROBINSON

TIL DEATH 3
BY ARYANNA

THE BIRTH OF A GANGSTER 4
BY DELMONT PLAYER

LAND OF THE HOOLIGANZ 3 | IRA B

PRODUCT OF THE STREETS 1&2
BY DEMOND "MONEY" ANDERSON

NO TIME FOR ERROR
BY KEESE

MONEY HUNGRY DEMONS
BY TRANAY ADAMS

Coming Soon from Lock Down Publications/Ca$h Presents

IF YOU CROSS ME ONCE 6
ANGEL V
By Anthony Fields

IMMA DIE BOUT MINE 4&5
By Aryanna

A THUGS STREET PRINCESS 3
By Meesha

PRODUCT OF THE STREETS 3
By Demond Money Anderson

CORNER BOYS
By Corey Robinson

SON OF A DOPE FIEND 4
By Renta

THE MURDER QUEENS 6&7
By Michael Gallon

CITY OF SMOKE 3
By Molotti

BETRAYAL OF A G
By Ray Vinci

CONFESSIONS OF A DOPE BOY
By Nicholas Lock

THA TAKEOVER
By Keith Chandler

Available Now

RESTRAINING ORDER 1 & 2
By **CA$H & Coffee**

LOVE KNOWS NO BOUNDARIES 1-3
By **Coffee**

RAISED AS A GOON I, II, III & IV
BRED BY THE SLUMS I, II, III
BLAST FOR ME I & II
ROTTEN TO THE CORE I II III
A BRONX TALE I, II, III
DUFFLE BAG CARTEL I II III IV V VI
HEARTLESS GOON I II III IV V
A SAVAGE DOPEBOY I II
DRUG LORDS I II III
CUTTHROAT MAFIA I II
KING OF THE TRENCHES
By **Ghost**

LAY IT DOWN I & II
LAST OF A DYING BREED I II
BLOOD STAINS OF A SHOTTA I & II III
By **Jamaica**

LOYAL TO THE GAME I II III
LIFE OF SIN I, II III
By **TJ & Jelissa**

IF LOVING HIM IS WRONG…I & II
LOVE ME EVEN WHEN IT HURTS I II III
By **Jelissa**

LAND OF THE HOOLIGANZ 3 | IRA B

BLOODY COMMAS I & II
SKI MASK CARTEL I, II & III
KING OF NEW YORK I II, III IV V
RISE TO POWER I II III
COKE KINGS I II III IV V
BORN HEARTLESS I II III IV
KING OF THE TRAP I II
By **T.J. Edwards**

WHEN THE STREETS CLAP BACK I & II III
THE HEART OF A SAVAGE I II III IV
MONEY MAFIA I II
LOYAL TO THE SOIL I II III
By **Jibril Williams**

A DISTINGUISHED THUG STOLE MY HEART I II & III
LOVE SHOULDN'T HURT I II III IV
RENEGADE BOYS 1-4
PAID IN KARMA 1-3
SAVAGE STORMS 1-3
AN UNFORESEEN LOVE 1-3
BABY, I'M WINTERTIME COLD 1-3
A THUG'S STREET PRINCESS 1&2
By **Meesha**

A GANGSTER'S CODE 1-3
A GANGSTER'S SYN 1-3
THE SAVAGE LIFE 1-3
CHAINED TO THE STREETS 1-3
BLOOD ON THE MONEY 1-3
A GANGSTA'S PAIN 1-3
BEAUTIFUL LIES AND UGLY TRUTHS
CHURCH IN THESE STREETS
By **J-Blunt**

LAND OF THE HOOLIGANZ 3 | IRA B

PUSH IT TO THE LIMIT
By **Bre' Hayes**

BLOOD OF A BOSS 1-5
SHADOWS OF THE GAME
TRAP BASTARD
By **Askari**

THE STREETS BLEED MURDER 1-3
THE HEART OF A GANGSTA 1-3
By **Jerry Jackson**

CUM FOR ME 1-8
An LDP Erotica Collaboration

BRIDE OF A HUSTLA 1-3
THE FETTI GIRLS 1-3
CORRUPTED BY A GANGSTA 1-4
BLINDED BY HIS LOVE
THE PRICE YOU PAY FOR LOVE 1-3
DOPE GIRL MAGIC 1-3
By **Destiny Skai**

WHEN A GOOD GIRL GOES BAD
By **Adrienne**

A KINGPIN'S AMBITION
A KINGPIN'S AMBITION II
I MURDER FOR THE DOUGH
By **Ambitious**

THE COST OF LOYALTY 1-3
By **Kweli**

LAND OF THE HOOLIGANZ 3 | IRA B

A GANGSTER'S REVENGE 1-4
THE BOSS MAN'S DAUGHTERS 1-5
A SAVAGE LOVE 1&2
BAE BELONGS TO ME 1&2
A HUSTLER'S DECEIT 1-3
WHAT BAD BITCHES DO 1-3
SOUL OF A MONSTER 1-3
KILL ZONE
A DOPE BOY'S QUEEN 1-3
TIL DEATH 1-3
IMMA DIE BOUT MINE 1-3
By **Aryanna**

TRUE SAVAGE 1-7
DOPE BOY MAGIC 1-3
MIDNIGHT CARTEL 1-3
CITY OF KINGZ 1&2
NIGHTMARE ON SILENT AVE
THE PLUG OF LIL MEXICO 1&2
CLASSIC CITY
By **Chris Green**

A DOPEBOY'S PRAYER
By **Eddie "Wolf" Lee**

THE KING CARTEL 1-3
By **Frank Gresham**

THESE NIGGAS AIN'T LOYAL 1-3
By **Nikki Tee**

GANGSTA SHYT 1-3
By **CATO**

THE ULTIMATE BETRAYAL
By **Phoenix**

BOSS'N UP 1-3
By **Royal Nicole**

I LOVE YOU TO DEATH
By **Destiny J**

I RIDE FOR MY HITTA
I STILL RIDE FOR MY HITTA
By **Misty Holt**

LOVE & CHASIN' PAPER
By **Qay Crockett**

TO DIE IN VAIN
SINS OF A HUSTLA
By **ASAD**

BROOKLYN HUSTLAZ
By **Boogsy Morina**

BROOKLYN ON LOCK 1 & 2
By **Sonovia**

GANGSTA CITY
By **Teddy Duke**

A DRUG KING AND HIS DIAMOND 1-3
A DOPEMAN'S RICHES
HER MAN, MINE'S TOO 1&2
CASH MONEY HO'S
THE WIFEY I USED TO BE 1&2
PRETTY GIRLS DO NASTY THINGS
By **Nicole Goosby**

LIPSTICK KILLAH 1-3
CRIME OF PASSION 1-3
FRIEND OR FOE 1-3
By **Mimi**

TRAPHOUSE KING 1-3
KINGPIN KILLAZ 1-3
STREET KINGS 1&2
PAID IN BLOOD 1&2
CARTEL KILLAZ 1-3
DOPE GODS 1&2
By **Hood Rich**

STEADY MOBBN' 1-3
THE STREETS STAINED MY SOUL 1-3
By **Marcellus Allen**

WHO SHOT YA 1-3
SON OF A DOPE FIEND 1-3
HEAVEN GOT A GHETTO 1&2
SKI MASK MONEY 1&2
By **Renta**

GORILLAZ IN THE BAY 1-4
TEARS OF A GANGSTA 1/&2
3X KRAZY 1&2
STRAIGHT BEAST MODE 1&2
By **DE'KARI**

TRIGGADALE 1-3
MURDA WAS THE CASE 1-3
By **Elijah R. Freeman**

THE STREETS ARE CALLING
By **Duquie Wilson**

LAND OF THE HOOLIGANZ 3 | IRA B

SLAUGHTER GANG 1-3
RUTHLESS HEART 1-3
By **Willie Slaughter**

GOD BLESS THE TRAPPERS 1-3
THESE SCANDALOUS STREETS 1-3
FEAR MY GANGSTA 1-5
THESE STREETS DON'T LOVE NOBODY 1-2
BURY ME A G 1-5
A GANGSTA'S EMPIRE 1-4
THE DOPEMAN'S BODYGAURD 1&2
THE REALEST KILLAZ 1-3
THE LAST OF THE OGS 1-3
By **Tranay Adams**

MARRIED TO A BOSS 1-3
By **Destiny Skai & Chris Green**

KINGZ OF THE GAME 1-7
CRIME BOSS 1-3
By **Playa Ray**

FUK SHYT
By **Blakk Diamond**

DON'T F#CK WITH MY HEART 1&2
By **Linnea**

ADDICTED TO THE DRAMA 1-3
IN THE ARM OF HIS BOSS
By **Jamila**

LOYALTY AIN'T PROMISED 1&2
By **Keith Williams**

YAYO 1-4
A SHOOTER'S AMBITION 1&2
BRED IN THE GAME
By **S. Allen**

TRAP GOD 1-3
RICH $AVAGE 1-3
MONEY IN THE GRAVE 1-3
CARTEL MONEY
By **Martell Troublesome Bolden**

FOREVER GANGSTA 1&2
GLOCKS ON SATIN SHEETS 1&2
By **Adrian Dulan**

TOE TAGZ 1-4
LEVELS TO THIS SHYT 1&2
IT'S JUST ME AND YOU
By **Ah'Million**

KINGPIN DREAMS 1-3
RAN OFF ON DA PLUG
By **Paper Boi Rari**

CONFESSIONS OF A GANGSTA 1-4
CONFESSIONS OF A JACKBOY 1-3
CONFESSIONS OF A HITMAN
By **Nicholas Lock**

I'M NOTHING WITHOUT HIS LOVE
SINS OF A THUG
TO THE THUG I LOVED BEFORE
A GANGSTA SAVED XMAS
IN A HUSTLER I TRUST
By **Monet Dragun**

LAND OF THE HOOLIGANZ 3 | IRA B

QUIET MONEY 1-3
THUG LIFE 1-3
EXTENDED CLIP 1&2
A GANGSTA'S PARADISE
By **Trai'Quan**

CAUGHT UP IN THE LIFE 1-3
THE STREETS NEVER LET GO 1-3
By **Robert Baptiste**

NEW TO THE GAME 1-3
MONEY, MURDER & MEMORIES 1-3
By **Malik D. Rice**

CREAM 2-3
THE STREETS WILL TALK
By **Yolanda Moore**

LIFE OF A SAVAGE 1-4
A GANGSTA'S QUR'AN 1-4
MURDA SEASON 1-3
GANGLAND CARTEL 1-3
CHI'RAQ GANGSTAS 1-4
KILLERS ON ELM STREET 1-3
JACK BOYZ N DA BRONX 1-3
A DOPEBOY'S DREAM 1-3
JACK BOYS VS DOPE BOYS 1-3
COKE GIRLZ
COKE BOYS
SOSA GANG 1&2
BRONX SAVAGES
BODYMORE KINGPINS
BLOOD OF A GOON
By **Romell Tukes**

LAND OF THE HOOLIGANZ 3 | IRA B

THE STREETS MADE ME 1-3
By **Larry D. Wright**

CONCRETE KILLA 1-3
VICIOUS LOYALTY 1-3
By **Kingpen**

THE ULTIMATE SACRIFICE 1-6
KHADIFI
IF YOU CROSS ME ONCE 1-3
ANGEL 1-4
IN THE BLINK OF AN EYE
By **Anthony Fields**

THE LIFE OF A HOOD STAR
By **Ca$h & Rashia Wilson**

THE STREETS WILL NEVER CLOSE 1-3
By **K'ajji**

NIGHTMARES OF A HUSTLA 1-3
By **King Dream**

HARD AND RUTHLESS 1&2
MOB TOWN 251
THE BILLIONAIRE BENTLEYS 1-3
REAL G'S MOVE IN SILENCE
By **Von Diesel**

GHOST MOB
By **Stilloan Robinson**

MOB TIES 1-6
SOUL OF A HUSTLER, HEART OF A KILLER 1-3
GORILLAZ IN THE TRENCHES
By **SayNoMore**

LAND OF THE HOOLIGANZ 3 | IRA B

BODYMORE MURDERLAND 1-3
THE BIRTH OF A GANGSTER 1-4
By **Delmont Player**

FOR THE LOVE OF A BOSS 1&2
By **C. D. Blue**

KILLA KOUNTY 1-5
By **Khufu**

MOBBED UP 1-4
THE BRICK MAN 1-5
THE COCAINE PRINCESS 1-10
STEPPERS 1-3
SUPER GREMLIN 1-4
By **King Rio**

MONEY GAME 1&2
By **Smoove Dolla**

A GANGSTA'S KARMA 1-4
By **FLAME**

KING OF THE TRENCHES 1-3
By **GHOST & TRANAY ADAMS**

QUEEN OF THE ZOO 1&2
By **Black Migo**

GRIMEY WAYS 1-3
By **Ray Vinci**

XMAS WITH AN ATL SHOOTER
By **Ca$h & Destiny Skai**

LAND OF THE HOOLIGANZ 3 | IRA B

KING KILLA 1&2
By **Vincent "Vitto" Holloway**

BETRAYAL OF A THUG 1&2
By **Fre$h**

THE MURDER QUEENS 1-5
By **Michael Gallon**

FOR THE LOVE OF BLOOD 1-4
By **Jamel Mitchell**

HOOD CONSIGLIERE 1&2
NO TIME FOR ERROR
By **Keese**

PROTÉGÉ OF A LEGEND 1&2
LOVE IN THE TRENCHES 1&2
By **Corey Robinson**

BORN IN THE GRAVE 1-3
CRIME PAYS
By **Self Made Tay**

MOAN IN MY MOUTH
By **XTASY**

TORN BETWEEN A GANGSTER AND A GENTLEMAN
By **J-BLUNT & Miss Kim**

LOYALTY IS EVERYTHING 1-3
CITY OF SMOKE 1&2
By **Molotti**

HERE TODAY GONE TOMORROW 1&2
By **Fly Rock**

WOMEN LIE MEN LIE 1-4
FIFTY SHADES OF SNOW 1-3
STACK BEFORE YOU SPLURGE
GIRLS FALL LIKE DOMINOES
NAÏVE TO THE STREETS
By **ROY MILLIGAN**

PILLOW PRINCESS
By **S. Hawkins**

THE BUTTERFLY MAFIA 1-3
SALUTE MY SAVAGERY 1&2
By **Fumiya Payne**

THE LANE 1&2
By Ken-Ken Spence

THE PUSSY TRAP 1-5
By **Nene Capri**

DIRTY DNA
By **Blaque**

SANCTIFIED AND HORNY
by **XTASY**

BOOKS BY LDP'S CEO, CA$H

TRUST IN NO MAN
TRUST IN NO MAN 2
TRUST IN NO MAN 3
BONDED BY BLOOD
SHORTY GOT A THUG
THUGS CRY
THUGS CRY 2
THUGS CRY 3
TRUST NO BITCH
TRUST NO BITCH 2
TRUST NO BITCH 3
TIL MY CASKET DROPS
RESTRAINING ORDER
RESTRAINING ORDER 2
IN LOVE WITH A CONVICT
LIFE OF A HOOD STAR
XMAS WITH AN ATL SHOOTER

Printed in the USA
CPSIA information can be obtained
at www.ICGtesting.com
CBHW050023271024
16475CB00014BA/1158